The

Ghost

OF CLEOPATRA

July 14, 2019

To Vickie:
Hoping you will
also find literary
happiness with
your writing!

[signature]

The *Ghost* OF CLEOPATRA

EDMONIA LEWIS AND HER LOST MASTERPIECE

A Work of Historical Fiction

John Rice and Gail Tanzer

THE GHOST OF CLEOPATRA

Copyright © 2019 by John Rice and Gail Tanzer

ALL RIGHTS RESERVED. No part of this book may be used or reproduced in any manner whatsoever without written permission from the author.

All photographs and images used with permission.

Print ISBN: 9781098743468

For Diane.

PROLOGUE

WHAT IS CREATED CANNOT BE separated from the creator. I came back to life as a statue in the mid-nineteenth century. Mary Edmonia Lewis was my sculptor. Her background, experiences, and frustrations in life paralleled many of mine. She was the ideal artist to re-create me. Little did either of us know that my statue, masterpiece that it was, would meet more challenges than either Edmonia or I ever faced. Here is our story.

Cleopatra

PART ONE
ABANDONED

Mary Edmonia Lewis
Eighteen Years Old
1861

LYING ON THE SNOWY GROUND, I just wanted to sleep. I imagined the soft mound where my head rested was my pillow. As the cold crept into my flesh, it dulled the pain of my bleeding wounds and deep bruises. The places where my dress was torn felt even colder. I shivered and felt like I might freeze to death. I knew that the boys who did this to me had left me here to die. I wanted to get up but my legs no longer worked. My heart was hardly beating, and I could barely breathe. I sank deeper into the snow, longing for sleep to release me. But I couldn't drift off because of the bells—the alarm bells. Were they ringing for me? I slipped into a dark, cold place.

A while later, I heard voices and felt people picking me up and carrying me. Again, I went to the dark place.

The next thing I remember was my head resting on a real pillow and my eyes staring at a ceiling. I looked around the room and saw the plain white walls where the only picture was Jesus knocking at a door. I realized I was in my room at Oberlin College.

My eyes closed. Somewhere between sleep and wakefulness, I experienced what I thought was a terrible nightmare. I was walking to the outhouse when a group of tall boys came out of nowhere. The mouth of one of the boys snarled a curse, but in my dream, I could not hear what he said. Before I could say anything, two of the boys grabbed my arms, and two others picked up my legs. I kicked with all my might and yelled.

They brought me to a field down the block from my rooming house, where they hoped no one would hear me screaming. A big boy with blonde hair and yellow eyes was shouting at me. There must have been seven or eight of them, all laughing and looking like the evil spirits my family had warned me about.

They formed a circle around me. Their faces were angry and they were shouting at me but I could not hear what they were saying.

They all set upon me at once. One yanked off my Ojibwe necklace. All its purple and white beads, of so much value to my mother, fell to the ground. Another tried to yank my pinafore down from my shoulder. No matter how much I tried to pull away, he succeeded. When another hiked up my skirt, I kicked him hard, but this only got him angrier.

The pain of one pulling my hair and kicking me in the back brought me to my knees, then onto the snow. Mercifully, everything went white.

～✺～

Half-asleep in my room, I wondered, Why didn't Auntie put out the dream catcher to capture that bad dream? Where were my father's totems, those spirits born in Africa that had often comforted me?

When I lived with my Ojibwe family and it was time

to go to sleep, I felt protected. Especially when I looked up and saw the dream catcher hanging from the birch bark ceiling.

My mother explained why dream catchers have so much power: a famous spirit, Spider Woman, watched over us Ojibwe children. When our people spread out over a long distance, she instructed the women of the clans to make hoops of willow and webbing, and embed them with beads. The webbing caught the bad dreams. A small hole allowed good dreams to come through. Feathers under the web let them trickle down to a child as comfort. With all my heart and soul, I believed in the power of the dream catcher!

Stabbing pains in my legs woke me up, and I stayed awake this time. Someone had dressed me in my nightshirt. I looked at an ugly bruise and bandages on my arms. Now I knew this wasn't just a nightmare.

I felt so alone.

Then I heard a voice; "You have me, Mary. You will always have me."

Where was the voice coming from? Shakily, I propped myself up on my elbows. I turned my aching neck left and right but couldn't see anyone.

My teeth chattered. "Who? Who is it? Did you say something?"

Most people in the modern world do not believe in ghosts or spirits. But in my day in Egypt, we knew that everyone has a ka or spirit. The ka of a deceased pharaoh was the most powerful. If a satisfactory statue were made after death, the pharaoh's ka would reside in it peacefully throughout eternity. But, if unhappy with the statue, the pharaoh's spirit would wander through time until it found a new, more suitable likeness.

Cleopatra

The first statue made of me was stiff and drab. Its black basalt was bleak. I wanted my new statue to capture my lively spirit. My ka wandered for centuries looking for just the right sculptor. When it found a child with roots in Africa whose mother possessed artistic talent, I got interested. Unfortunately, that poor child felt abandoned after her beating at Oberlin---but she was never alone.

I was always with Mary Edmonia to help her develop the talent and desire to eventually sculpt me. It took time, occasional ghostly appearances like the one at Oberlin, and unexpected help from other spirits, but it finally led to her making my new statue—The Death of Cleopatra.

The Statue—The Death of Cleopatra

THE YEAR IS 1972, AND I feel abandoned, just like Mary Edmonia Lewis felt at Oberlin. The Queen of the Nile is sinking deep into the mud. I am reclined on my throne, in the final spasm of death, my right hand still clutching the serpent. My flesh is the finest Carrara marble, but my features are damaged or missing. My once-perfect complexion has become "sugary," roughened by exposure to wind and rain for 70-odd years. My once-magnificent nose is smashed away, and a big chunk is missing from my noble chin. My delicate sandals have weathered, as have the royal hands that once ruled Egypt, and the feet that bestrode an empire.

I am sinking in the mud of an excavating company, under the leaden skies of Cicero, Illinois. The air is filled with smoke and nature's own gloom. The clank-clank-clank of a nearby forge fills the air. I'm surrounded by rusting hulks: bulldozers, front-end loaders, and dump trucks, vehicles that will never move again, their engines scavenged for parts.

Other vehicles rumble in and out of the yard. They make me quiver and shake and cause me to sink deeper into the mud. After parking their vehicles, the drivers sprawl on my lap. They think it's funny to sit on the Queen. They don't know who I am, exactly. They don't know who carved me. They have no idea what I have been through.

They first met me in Forest Park. They had a

government contract to dig a foundation for a post office, and I was smack in the middle of the dig. The workers draped me in chains and used a front-end loader to hoist me onto the bed of a lowboy truck. I didn't seem worth saving. Graffiti scarred and marred my breasts. Blue paint disfigured my face. Decades of abuse had left deep stains. I had a bit of beauty left, but it was well concealed under layers of dirt.

Normally, a piece of "junk" like me would be shipped to a landfill. But, as evidenced by the old hulks around me, this company didn't throw anything away. They didn't know what do with me. So, they lowered me onto the muddy ground at the rear of the yard and removed the chains. Not one of the workers knew I was a lost masterpiece the world had been missing for a hundred years. Even the bosses didn't know, but they for some reason, couldn't bear to part with me.

Cleopatra

MY SPIRIT WAS NOT ALWAYS captured in stone. My form was once flesh and blood. I was not the first Cleopatra. No, that was Alexander's beloved sister. He conquered my country three hundred years before I was born. He gave Egypt as a reward to his most trusted general, Ptolemy. That's my father's name, too.

My family, like Alexander's, was from Macedonia. We built a splendid city bearing his name in our new land. From there, we ruled our subjects like the pharaohs before us. We were gods. We treated our subjects cruelly, yet they worshipped us.

My father was a harsh ruler, like every leader of our dynasty. He spoiled his five children with gifts while his subjects starved. I was his favorite. I think it's because I had his prominent nose and strong chin. My skin was darker, though, like my Egyptian mother. She was softer than my father and had a heart for her people. Her name was also Cleopatra.

I was not pretty. My brown eyes were too far apart and deeply recessed. My mouth was small and my lips anything but sensuous. I wore my brown hair pulled back into a simple bun. Physical beauty wasn't as important to me as it was to my sisters. It wasn't earned, although some put a lot of work into it. It could also lead to heartache: a smart young woman recognized only for her beauty forced into a loveless marriage. The people I loved most had the angular features of Ptolemy.

I had inherited more from my father than just his looks. He played the flute and devoured art and music. He listened to the learned philosophers of our age. He hired tutors for each of his children. None of my siblings took their lessons seriously. Learning was my greatest delight.

My tutors taught me literature, art, music, and medicine. Philostratos taught me philosophy and rhetoric. He was a frail man with a thin voice, but he mesmerized me. He taught me the power of speech. Though I was shy inside, he forced me to recite classic speeches under his critical gaze. He corrected me constantly and insisted I relax, making me even more nervous.

"Cleopatra, no one will listen to you unless your bearing and voice command them," he would chide. "Don't cross your feet when you stand, but plant them apart like you own this Earth. Don't fidget, but use your hands"—he pumped his scrawny arm—"to strengthen your words. Stop looking down," he commanded. "Look into my eyes until you're staring at my soul. When you speak to crowds, as I'm sure you'll do one day, focus on the ones in front of you—choose one on the left, one in the center, and one on your right. Command them not to look away, as you pour out your words."

His training turned me into a speaker who drew every eye and ear. But, unlike my ancestors, I was not content to speak only in my native tongue. No, I wanted to speak to my people, like my mother did, in her gentle tone. Though we had ruled this land for three centuries, I was the first of my family to speak the language of Egypt.

I also learned the languages of four other countries that comprised our vast empire. Our family ruled the lands surrounding the sea, back when Rome was only a rumor. Ha! They call their capital the Eternal City. Those upstarts with their ruthless ways. There is only one Eternal City—Alexandria!

Mary Edmonia Lewis

AFTER I HEARD THE VOICE calling me, I was met only with ghostly silence, I fell back on my pillow and helplessly stared at the ceiling.

"Mrs. Keep, Mrs. Keep!" I yelled, hoping my house-mother was around.

She burst into the room.

"Mary, you're awake!"

"Did you hear someone talking?" My voice was trembling.

"No, Mary. Maybe you were dreaming. I was in the next room. No one has come by."

I tried to forget about the voice. "Did I . . . how did I get beaten up?"

"Do not trouble yourself; you're going to be all right."

"But . . . but . . . what happened?"

Mrs. Keep sighed. "A terrible thing."

"Who did it?"

My housemother settled down on a simple wooden chair next to my bed. She took my hand into her soft, cold one. It hurt me to be touched even so slightly. Maybe the boys tried to crush my hands along with my spirit. But the desire for tenderness outweighed the pain of her touch. I let Mrs. Keep hold my hand.

"It was because of the girls, right?" I wanted to know.

"Try not to trouble yourself." Mrs. Keep patted me on my forehead. "Anyhow, you certainly did not deserve this."

Tears welled up in her eyes as she studied my swollen face. "You haven't eaten for two days."

"Have I been sleeping that long?"

"I don't know if I would call it sleep. You have just been away for a while."

It was difficult to keep my eyes open, but I wanted to look into Mrs. Keep's to understand what she meant about "being away." My Ojibwe people didn't look each other straight in the eye. It was like invading a person's soul. But, since I had been living with white people, I did a lot of things differently.

"Where was I?"

"I'll bring you some soup. Try to sit up, dear."

When she returned, my housemother sank a spoon into a bowl of carrot soup and lifted it to my mouth. I managed to swallow until I finished half the bowl.

"Thanks," I yawned, and settled back.

Mrs. Keep rearranged the covers around me. I faded away again until I felt someone tug my blanket and whisper, "Mary, Mary."

Opening my eyes, I saw Clara gazing down at me. Tall, slender, and serious looking, she was my best friend. What made Clara special was her willingness to listen. She also had the common sense that I envied. She liked me because I made her loosen up and laugh.

"Are you going to stay in that bed forever?"

I tried to sit up. It hurt my back. "You would think I had drunk wine," I laughed.

"This is no time for jokes," Clara said, solemnly.

"What do you mean?" I teased. Clara talked about the pranks I had pulled in school and the medicine pouch I carried to "cast spells."

There was a long silence.

"I know I did those things, but the girl who believed in dream catchers and spirits protecting me . . . she's gone."

"Why did you poison Christina and Maria?" she suddenly asked.

I winced. "I didn't poison those girls!"

"Well," Clara continued, "They aren't back from

break yet, but word is you served them spiced wine before they went sledding with their fellows. They both became ill: they almost died."

Clara sighed. "Were you angry you couldn't go home for break? Or jealous? Was that why you did it."

I was firm. "I was feeling sorry for myself but I didn't poison those girls. Don't you believe me?"

"Of course, I wouldn't be here if I didn't. I had to sneak here, so the girls wouldn't catch me associating with you."

Silence hung over the room like a dark cloud.

It burst, and I could not hold back my tears.

"Why am I so different? Other girls have parents. They have beaus."

Clara squeezed my hand.

"I don't fit with the white people or the Negro ones. People think I'm colored but I feel pure Ojibwe, and there aren't any Indian boys here. The colored boys sing in their own choir, songs from the plantations. I can hardly understand their words. Not that my English is that great."

"It's improved."

"Yes, but I'll never be one for fancy words, and that's fine with me."

I felt myself slipping towards sleep but wanted to finish my thoughts. "Besides, I may never trust a boy again, after what happened in that field."

I turned my head to the wall.

"Please don't let those boys sour you on all fellows. Someday we'll get married, to fine young men."

I was half-listening to Clara as my eyes closed. I slept

until nightfall. I awakened to thoughts about Maria and Christina. I felt badly for them, but I had it worse. I had no parents to turn to in my time of need. I didn't have a boyfriend or girlfriend, except for Clara.

The rat-tat-tat of rain pelting the roof interrupted my thoughts. A bolt of lightning struck so loudly I sat up as straight as an arrow.

A white ribbon rushed through the slightly open window. The ribbon grew wider and took the shape of a person sitting on what looked like a throne. The throne had lions' heads on its arms.

It was hard to separate the filmy white figure from the white walls of the room, but there was a rippling that defined its outline. Although the figure was hazy, I could tell it was a woman. Sitting and staring straight ahead in a prideful way, she looked like an ancient queen. She wore a long, tight dress, and held a scepter. A headpiece with what looked like a bird was her crown.

I squeaked, "Who are you? What do you want?"

The figure moved around in a wavy sort of way, giving off a feeling of cold air.

I was panicking. "What—what do you want?" I heard myself demand again.

The queen on her throne traveled around the room about five times, going up towards the ceiling and down towards the floor, but always returning to the end of my bed. I forced myself to get up. I walked towards the woman, but when I tried to touch her she dissolved into a smoky trail and went out the window.

The voice coming from nowhere. Now the ghostly

figure. This was not the first time I had experienced such strange things. And I feared it would not be the last.

The Statue

IT'S 1972. I WOULD CONTINUE to shake and sink for the next nine years, as the earth movers rumbled past. Then something changed. I still shook, but trucks of a different kind drove past. These were bulky and loud and gave off an unforgettable stench. They pulled into the lot and sat on the scale. Then they drove into a building, where they dumped their foul contents—banana peels, coffee grounds, all the fermenting waste of urban life.

Thanks to the new owner, I had some company. At night, rats scampered across my face and perched on my royal headdress. They twitched and squealed, but there was nothing to eat on my marble body. So, they crawled through holes in the building to fight for scraps on the concrete. This new enterprise was a garbage transfer facility.

A mother and son operated it. They occasionally salvaged something useful from the waste, but most of it was shipped to a landfill.

They thought of having me shipped to the mountain of garbage, but something stopped them. For three more years, I sat there, a curiosity. No one knew who I was, or what to do with me. Then, one day, it was time for a fire inspection. Cicero's Fire Inspector, Harold Adams, was making his yearly visit. With Harold, it was more a social call than an official one.

He entered the office and greeted Lorraine, who was at her desk working on the accounts. She was a 60-year-old petite blond. Her father had started the company and she gave all her attention to bookkeeping, and was careful not to interfere with operations. Her son Dan was now in charge of that.

"It's that time of year again," Harold said, as he sat down in the small office. He was a trim 47-year-old, resplendent in his navy blue suitcoat and pants offsetting his crisp white shirt. It was too hot for him to wear his uniform cap. Black-rimmed glasses framed his square face and matched his dark hair.

"Harry," she said warmly, "I just made some coffee."

"I had mine this morning," he responded, "But I'll take a cup." Harold never turned down anything free. She handed him a Styrofoam cup brimming with strong, dark coffee.

"Where's Dan?"

"He's working the front loader."

"I can see business is booming," Harold said, as another truck pulled onto the scale.

Lorraine beamed. "That's one thing about garbage—it's never slow."

He took a sip and stood up. "Well, I can see your fire extinguisher is in the right place." He walked over, turned it upside down, and glanced at the sticker. "And it's up to date. Guess I'll take a quick look around. Tell Dan I'm here if he's not too busy."

Harold walked into the yard, not looking at anything in particular, just taking in a summer afternoon. He playfully stomped on the scale. He enjoyed being outdoors and having breezy conversations with the business owners. The only thing he loved more than conversation was watching documentaries and reading history books. Harold had a love of old objects and the stories behind them.

He strolled toward the back of the lot and saw me, the Queen of the Nile, sitting in the mud, enshrouded in a layer of brown dust. He would later say I was like "a great white ghost" crying out for rescue. He stepped carefully around puddles to reach me. He examined me from every angle. Harold saw me as worth saving. He was the rare man who could sense my majesty.

PART TWO
BIRTH

Mary Edmonia Lewis
1844 - 1850
Birth to Six Years Old

FROM THE TIME I WAS a small child I began hearing, feeling, and seeing things that others didn't. When I was born, it was 1844 or 1845. I'm not sure, because our little town of Greenbush, New York, didn't make people get birth certificates. When I got older and people asked me when I was born, I wavered about the year, but I would always give the date as July 4, because that was easy to remember.

Our family didn't celebrate birthdays. But, during boring evenings in the long, cold winters, they loved to tell stories. One of these was the story of my birth, which they told using very simple English. My family spoke Creole and Ojibwe, but English was the language we could all understand.

My father was from Haiti, so he spoke Creole. My mother spoke Ojibwe. My 12-year-old half-brother Samuel spoke Creole, but at his mission school he had to speak English, which was my main language.

I heard that I was born on a summer day and it was hot in our one-room cabin. My aunties helped bring me into the world by chanting together their Ojibwe prayers. When I came, they celebrated with a happy yipping sound. One of them ran to my uncle's wigwam where my father and brother stayed during the whole ordeal.

My aunt told them Mother and I were healthy. My

father Edmund asked, "Is it a boy?" He was a bit disappointed to hear, "No, but she is beautiful."

"That is fine, but I want her to have my name."

After my parents thought about it for a week, they named me Mary Edmonia (for my father) and gave me his last name, Lewis.

Catherine was my mother, and my aunts were Elizabeth and Sarah. They were Ojibwe, but their mother gave them English names, because my Negro grandfather couldn't pronounce Ojibwe names.

My uncles had Ojibwe names. One uncle was Namyd (Star Dancer) and the other was Ogima (Chief). Ogima lived up to his name: he was the unspoken head of our group.

Every day my father went to work as a "gentleman's servant." He told us about all the fancy things his boss owned: store-bought furniture, horses, carriages, etc. He was proud to work in such a fine home.

"My boss treats me well," Papa said, "And pays me just enough to make the rent on our house."

When he spoke like this, my nimaamaa (Ojibwe for mother) would complain, "You took me away from Niagara Falls."

Papa would look to see if regret had crept into my mother's eyes. "I couldn't live like your family, freezing in wigwams. You said that as long as your sisters and their families came along, you would be happy, isn't that right?"

My mother never disappointed him. She always said with the slightest of smiles, "That is right."

My parents had met at Niagara Falls, which my mother insisted on calling "Thunder Waters." I couldn't picture the place. My mother lived there with two aunts and uncles. The women sold beaded moccasins and clothes, while the men hunted and fished.

My father was selling tickets for the tour boats at the bottom of the Falls. He saw my nimaamaa selling her goods to tourists. She spoke kindly with the tourists and looked lovely with her long, braided hair and pretty eyes. My father said he fell in love with her sweet voice. He invited her to take a ride on the tour boat. They got married within a few months. My father said it was the best decision he ever made.

~⊘~

One day, he found me playing with some objects on a table in the corner. He took them from me and said he used them in his voodoo religion.

"What is religion?" I asked.

Pap thought for a while. "it's a way we think about the being who created us. We from Haiti call him the Supreme Being."

"Like nimaamaa's Great Spirit or our priest's God?" I asked.

Pap smiled. "Yes. The Supreme Being is so busy he has spirits helping him out. They are called Lwa. My favorite Lwa is Legba, or Lazarus. See that picture of him on the table leaning against the wall.

I had looked at it many times before. "That Lazarus looks like he needs help himself."

`My father laughed. "I know he's walking with a cane, but he's the only man who came back from the dead. That makes him strong. With his special power, he brings my prayers to the Supreme Being."

We just sat there quietly, me on his lap, looking at his treasures.

Then Papa said, "And another thing, my Lwa brings me messages in my dreams. The dreams warn me about things to come—sometimes good, sometimes bad."

"Dreams are very important," my mother chimed in.

Some of my dreams were scary. I changed the subject. "What is that cross with chains next to your table?"

"That old cross stands for another Lwa named Baron Samedi . . . how do I explain him, Samuel?"

My brother Samuel was reading. Like my father, Samuel was slim, had brown-black skin, and sparkling white teeth. But he was also different from my papa. Samuel kept his tightly curled hair short and neat, and he always tucked in his shirt. My papa let his grayish-black hair get wild at times, and he didn't care if the back of his shirt flew in the wind. That is, until my mother would make him tidy up before he went to work.

It took a moment for Samuel to turn his head from what he was reading. "What, Papa?"

"Could you tell about the cross to Mary? It is hard for me to say in English."

"My real mommy told me that Baron Samedi is a Lwa that guides us through the crossroads of life, when we go from one place to another. Like from the Falls to Greenbush. Or even from life to death."

"Why the chains?" I asked.

This subject made Papa angry. "The French made my people slaves! My first people were from Africa. The French put them in chains and brought them to Haiti to work on their plantations."

I asked Papa if he had been a slave.

He stood up, making me slide off his lap. He shook his fists and yelled, "Many of my ancestors died as slaves, but my people fought for their freedom and finally won, just before I was born!"

"You're scaring me, Papa."

"I'm sorry, Mary, I just wanted you to know."

Calming himself, Papa told me about other things in his corner: how the candle honored God, and the dried beetles and leaves made people well.

Papa motioned to his corner. "One more thing, Mary. See that drum there? When I drum by myself, I call to my Lwa, and he tells me things."

"Like what?"

"He helped me find the right words to ask your nimaamaa to marry me." With that, Papa winked at me as well as at my mother, and Nimaamaa nodded back to him.

❧

One night, long after we had gone to bed, I heard my mother scream. My brother and I sat up in our beds on the platform above my parents.

I sleepily asked what was wrong.

Samuel jumped down and yelled, "Papa, Papa!"

When I climbed down, I saw my mother shaking my

father and yelling for him to wake up. He didn't move. He lay still as a stone, with his eyes wide open.

I sat in a corner, hugging my knees against my chest. My heart was beating so hard I felt it would jump from my chest. I watched as my mother and Samuel tried to shake my father back to life. They finally gave up.

"What will happen to Papa?" I begged.

"Don't bother me with questions," Nimaamaa said. She was sobbing.

Samuel sat next to Papa, grabbing his lifeless hand and crying like a lost child.

When I climbed the ladder back to my bed, I heard a soft wind, and then rain falling on our tin roof. Even the skies cried when my papa died.

~~∾⊙∾~~

The next day, my mother dressed me in a long skirt and a white blouse she had bought at the French trading post.

Nimaamaa opened a painted, dried piece of hide that she called a parfleche. It held her best beadwork. She pulled out a necklace with several layers of purple and white bead, the same necklace the boys would rip off me at Oberlin. She told me these colors were hard to come by, which made these beads valuable.

As her tears dropped on my hair, she slipped the necklace over my head.

From a birch bark container, my mother pulled out a sash adorned with flower designs that she had made for me. She put the sash over my shoulder. She handed me the red handkerchief that Papa kept in his trouser pocket. "Here, Mary. Your papa believed if you wear red it keeps away the spirits of the dead that could come looking for you."

I groaned.

Nimaamaa put on the wedding dress she had made for herself seven years earlier. She had sewn shells and dyed porcupine quills onto the deerskin. On her feet, she wore her finest beaded moccasins.

Samuel wore his cleanest dark breeches and white shirt. The three of us walked to my papa's church.

My mother took my hand and put her arm through Samuel's. My aunties, uncles, and four little cousins, dressed in their best deerskin clothing, met us along the way. Over their shoulders, they carried their fanciest bags, and my uncles carried their painted drums.

My uncles and aunties also carried long pieces of birch bark. When we came next to them, I could see there was something lying on the wood. There, on top of the birch bark, all dressed in his Sunday best, was my father! I thought I would faint.

Somehow, I kept up as we walked to the little Jesuit church where my father had taken Samuel and me so many times. The young priest, Father Clement, greeted us with a solemn smile. He then did much crossing and sprinkling of water over Papa's body. The strong smell of incense came from a smoking bowl that Father swung over my dead papa's body.

Father Clement cleared his throat and said, "Edmund Lewis worked hard, was a good family man, and came often to Mass. A man like Edmund will probably go to a wonderful place called heaven. But, in case he has to stop in an unpleasant place called purgatory, please pray his stay will be short."

He must have noticed that my mother, Samuel, and I winced, because he added, "But, as I said, Edmund will probably feel God's embrace right away--- he was such a good man."

Raising both of his arms over Papa and the rest of us, Father said, "May the Lord Jesus bless and keep you. Amen."

As we walked from the church, my aunt Sarah tied a leather strap around the wrist of each of us children. I asked her why.

Aunt Sarah answered, "Those straps tell the spirits you children are still attached to the earth, so they won't get any ideas of taking you away with your father." I gave her a sour look.

The men carried Papa on his birch bark bed, and the grown-ups became silent. Our quiet little group got looks from our white neighbors along the road. Standing on their stoops, some took off their hats. They held them to their chest and bowed their heads.

When we came to our house, Nimaamaa said to Samuel, "Go get that old cross. Oh, and Lazarus."

Samuel did as she said, and we all crowded into Auntie's wigwam. Inside the dome-shaped home, Uncle Ogima motioned for us to sit.

He looked at Papa's body and proclaimed in Ojibwe, "Dear Edmund Lewis, the Great Spirit has taken you. You now go to a better place, but your journey may be hard. An evil spirit may surprise you on your path, but stay strong. There are good spirits who will help."

Uncle paused and then continued, "When you make it to your new world, Edmund, you will see your dead relatives. They will ask about the people still living. Tell them Mary and Samuel are not ready to come."

Nimaamaa put her arm around us.

Mournful sounds came from my aunts and uncles.

I whispered to my mother, "Why these noises?"

"To make Papa fly quickly to his dead family and not bring any of us with him."

I gulped.

Then my uncles cut a hole in the back wall. I asked what it was for.

Nimaamaa whispered, "Because if his body goes out the main door your father may stay a ghost and come back to haunt us."

I shivered.

My mother opened a pouch. She took out a silver rosary, Papa's white gloves, her finest beads, and a locket worn by Papa's dead first wife. She laid them on my father's chest.

As if on signal, my uncles carried Papa outside.

Together we walked to a small, cleared plot of land in the woods. Someone had already dug up a large patch of dirt. My uncles slowly lowered Papa's body into it. Lengths of birch bark lay near the grave. My aunties used it to cover my papa's body. Off to the side was a long, low thing that looked like a birch bark house. My uncles had made it.

They grabbed both ends of the house and raised it over Papa.

It seemed so final. My papa, covered, forever. I found myself screaming, "That's not Papa's house. He belongs in my house, with me!"

Everyone stared at me. Nimaamaa commanded, "Mary, you must be quiet."

"No, I won't. The Great Spirit can't take my father. He's mine!"

Finally, Uncle Namyd came over to me, patted me on my shoulder and said, "Be calm, Mary. The Great Spirit knows when to take people."

"No, he doesn't. It's not time yet!"

My solemn, brave family didn't know how to handle me. I sank to my knees next to the house and wailed.

Samuel pulled my arm and walked me away. He crouched down and faced me. "Mary, Papa doesn't want you to cry. I'll take care of you. You'll be all right." He said this while tears ran down his cheeks.

I finally caught my breath and said, "Okay," and walked back to where they were burying my father. I had to try really hard to keep from running. While my people chanted, I squeezed my eyes shut, so I couldn't see the little house over my father's body.

Nimaamaa whispered to Samuel, "Put the cross in the ground."

I heard Samuel grunt as he pushed the cross into the dirt so that it would stay straight. I prayed Baron Samedi would guard Papa on his journey.

Then Samuel put the picture of Lazarus on the spirit house. My mother said to the group, "Edmund believed his Lwa would protect him wherever he went."

Suddenly, I felt a burst of wind.

My eyes flew open, and I pulled Samuel's shirtsleeve. "Did you feel that?"

"What?" he asked.

"Like a strong wind in winter."

"You're just imagining things," he said, gently.

∽⊚∾

The next day, I said to my mother, "I felt the spirit taking Papa."

"Hmm. I didn't feel it."

Oh, well, if no one else believed me, it would be a little secret to share with my papa.

"But where will Papa go now?"

"Your papa will get to a land where he will hear drumming and singing. There will be fruits and fish—a feast. And your papa will see his parents and grandparents and all who went before him."

My mother motioned for me to help her put food on the table.

"No!" I said.

I wasn't used to disobeying my mother, but I pouted and stayed right where I was. Finally, though, I went to her. She opened her arms and I buried my face in her thick middle.

Some days later, Samuel packed his clothes to return to school. "It won't be long 'til I graduate. I'll find a job. Who knows, Mary, I may become rich. When I do, I will help you and mother."

It was soon time for us to pack our belongings. The owner of our little rented house knew we had hardly any money. He said we could stay for one more month without paying him. When we closed the door on our cabin for the last time, I cried.

Uncle Ogima and Aunt Sarah said we could stay in their wigwam. It was strange sleeping on the earth instead of a wooden floor, even though Auntie made me a soft bed of pine boughs and covered it with deerskin. It also seemed strange to be living with so many people in one small space. Crowded into the wigwam were my aunt and uncle, their six-year-old daughter, Abequa, and their six–

month-old baby, my uncle's mother, Nokomis, along with my mother and me. Where would Samuel sleep, when he returned?

At night, we all slept with our heads towards the wall and our feet facing the center, where, on cool nights, Nokomis made a fire. There was a round opening in the roof to let out the smoke.

Nimaamaa worked from dawn to dark, sewing beads on moccasins and flower designs on sashes.

I asked her why she was working so hard.

She said she needed to make more things to send with traders to sell at Thunder Waters. To me, she was working so hard to keep her sadness all neatly sewn up, so it wouldn't come undone.

As often as I could, I played outside with my cousins. We played scary games, pretending that big, bad Manitous chased us, but I didn't need a dreamcatcher, yet.

After a few months, Aunt Sarah said to my mother, "Maybe we should move back to the Falls? The hunting and fishing is good and you can sell your beadwork and sewing."

"I never thanked you for leaving the Falls, Sarah, to move here with me and my Edmund. You're right, we should go back home."

Home to them, but not to me, I snarled inside.

Then I heard something that made me want to run to the Falls too, even if they were full of thunder.

After a day of trading with the French, Uncle Ogima told us about a new law, The Fugitive Slave Act. It said that a person could be whipped or jailed for hiding a slave, or a child of a slave, in your home, or wigwam.

When she heard the news, my mother looked right at me.

"What . . . what's wrong, Nimaamaa? Did I do something?"

Mother said, "No, Mary, but I have to explain something to you."

She took a deep breath. "I didn't want this day to come." I knew we were on the verge of something big.

She explained all about slavery, but I calmly answered, "Oh, what Papa said—how they used to have slaves in Haiti."

"Yes, something like that. But they do that now, right here, and they could take you!"

"No!" I gasped.

Nimaamaa grabbed my hands and squeezed them. "You are Negro, like the slave people."

"What?" I cried.

"Ne . . . Nee . . . gro? I don't even know what that word means," I said.

"Some say 'colored.' You're colored brown like some slave people. Others are more like black. Look at your hands, then look at the rest of our hands."

Nimaamaa spoke gently but seriously. "You, Mary, are the darkest of us all."

This was the first of many times I would feel "different," like I didn't belong.

I cried. Abequa put her arm around me. I asked, "Am I bad? Is there something wrong with me?"

"No, Child. You are beautiful, but we want to keep you," my mother said.

Nimaamaa looked at everyone in our wigwam and declared, "It's time to go back to Thunder Waters on the Canada side, where they don't allow slaves."

Everyone nodded in agreement.

Uncle Ogima made it official; "We go back."

We packed our few belongings.

I wanted to get away, but one thing bothered me: I didn't want to leave my father behind. Then I remembered the gust of wind when we buried Papa, and I said to my mother, "Nimaamaa, you didn't believe me when I heard that sound when we buried Papa, but maybe that means his spirit left then?"

"Probably, but tell me if that happens again. The spirits may be talking to you, and that means you have a special gift."

I frowned. "But I don't want a special gift."

"You may not have a choice, Mary. The spirits choose you."

I groaned.

Then Mother said words that I would never forget; "I'll tell you one thing that's very important: there is more power in what we don't see than in what we do."

The Statue
1870

ALTHOUGH EDMONIA WAS BORN INTO humble conditions, she was deeply loved. At what I would call my "rebirth," no one particularly loved me, but I endured it all because this was my chance for immortality.

I was born far from this desolate place of Cicero, Illinois: not in an industrial landscape, but on a tree-covered mountain. The skies were the deepest azure, not this gray canopy. The sun was so bright, it hurt. It was warm; I wasn't pounded by blizzards and freezing rain. It was across an ocean, in a place called Carrara.

I was not born one hundred years ago, as some would say. It took millions of years to form my flesh. You could say I am 200 million years old. They would have called me limestone back then. But something special happened to me, only 27 million years ago: a plate of oceanic rocks from Corsica crashed into the boot of Italy.

For ten million years, the collisions continued. They buried me under six miles of rock. The temperature rose to 450 degrees Fahrenheit. The high heat converted me from soft, textured limestone to hard, smooth, glistening marble. I wouldn't be a mere brownstone, but a work of art. I could have ended up as a wall or floor of a cathedral. An altar, maybe. It all depended on what my creator chose.

But, first, there was much work to free me from my mountain. Men had been cutting slabs of marble from my mountain for centuries. They were called cavatori. These were rough characters. They worked all day in the hot sun and drowned in wine when the cool evening came. They were unafraid to strike if their pay wasn't proper. They hated their bosses, or, for that matter, any kind of authority. They were outcasts, as I would become.

The cavatori stood in a line on top of the mountainside.

They wore hats or scarfs to keep the sun off. They wore heavy hemp ropes around their waists to keep from falling. Using picks, they dug a narrow trench along the top of the mountain face. Then they swung their sledgehammers to drive iron wedges to separate me from my mountain.

It was dangerous, dirty work. The white dust they breathed would slowly kill them. But it was far more likely their death would be sudden and bloody. Slabs of marble could crash down on men working on the quarry floor. Drivers could be crushed by the wheels of carts. Runaway slabs could slice right through a work crew. It's no surprise the men were fatalistic and fearless, and no strangers to violence away from the quarry.

Government officials considered them a political cancer eating away at their laws and institutions. Bosses were wary of being caught alone by the cavatori. The men figured they would die on the job, anyway. Why not take a boss or a policeman along for the final ride?

Still, they were dedicated to the work itself, and took pride in their superhuman ability to harvest a substance as hard and delicate as me.

While the line of cavatori pounded their wedges deeper and deeper, teams of men in the quarry pulled on long heavy ropes to free my slab. They were using ancient methods that had improved little since the Romans had found the marble and quarried it to build their Eternal City. Muscle, sweat, hammers, ropes, wedges: sheer human determination was still the way they did it.

When they finally freed me, I left behind a smooth face, for the next cut. The men allowed giant slabs, like me, to crash onto the quarry floor, since no amount of men could hold my weight. I broke into jagged, irregular pieces, with a few semi-square blocks. There was still so much work.

Men pulled two-man gang saws back and forth over my marble surface, the blade sinking a tiny bit each time. It would take days for the team to cut away my excess stone, to make me a square. Then men attacked my "love handles" with chisels to knock off offending outcroppings. Then some other artisans sanded and smoothed my complexion. Scabblers was their name. They were akin to plastic surgeons. They removed any ugly abnormalities and left behind gleaming flesh.

Finished, I was loaded onto a lizza, a kind of sled made from the sturdiest of wood. The men had created paths for these lizzas to slide down. The paths were paved with greased poles, laid side by side, like railroad ties.

Ropes were tied to the lizza and a team of men kept it from it careening down the path. The ropes were as thick as the arms of the men who strained against them. They slowed my descent to a safe speed. As the lizza slid over the poles, another crew took the ones from in back and placed them in front. They moved me as close to the road as possible, to be loaded onto a wagon.

It was now the job of the teamsters to fasten ropes around me and hoist me onto their wagon. There was a tense moment, when I could have come crashing down on them and splintered their wagon.

Hitched to my wagon was a large team of oxen, more than 20. The weight they pulled! I was so enormous. Many oxen died instantly in their traces.

I was lying there in the wagon. I must have weighed 3,500 pounds, at least. Sitting in the front seat were my two drivers, Carlo Lentino and Giuseppe Luchessi. Though they cursed each other continually, as well as the stubborn team, they were cousins, united in their political beliefs. Both came from the same village in Campania and from a long line of cavatori.

Carlo's grandfather, Enrico, had started working in the quarry as a young boy. He got too close to a wagon and one of the oxen kicked him in his left leg. The blow snapped Enrico's femur. He limped around on that shortened leg the rest of his life, until a stroke took him at 54.

Giuseppe was the fourth generation of his family to mine marble. His father and uncles had all died in their thirties from breathing in the lethal dust. That's why he chose to drive a wagon rather than work in the quarry, and he always wore a red handkerchief over his mouth. His nickname was "Bandit."

The two friends were both part of a secret society called Anarchia. They hoped one day to overthrow the deceitful government. They longed for a new day when they would be on the same social level as their cruel bosses. They dreamed of a paradise of socialist equality, where there would be opportunities for smart men like them to escape the quarry.

They didn't discuss such things as they started their six-mile journey to the port of Luna. Carlo held the reins and whipped the oxen mercilessly. The sullen animals barely reacted to the lash but kept lumbering along. Giuseppe's job was to jump off to remove obstacles, or to free the wagon from mud. When they got stuck, he would stick a long pole under a wheel and use all his strength and weight to lift it above the mire.

The day they hauled me it was sunny and dry, and, although several oxen fell to their knees, none died. "Where's this one going?" Carlo asked Giuseppe. His partner glanced at the bill of sale; "Roma."

"Of course," Carlo said, slapping his weathered forehead, "It's going to a great artist. The artist will make something beautiful and it will sit in a rich person's home."

"Yes," Giuseppe agreed, "How many loaves of bread, how many families could be fed with the money that will be paid for this?" He went on, contemptuously; "A cold piece of marble is not worth more than the life of one peasant. Yet many peasants die in the quarry. Someday, you and I, our numbers will be up."

"Maybe yours," Carlo laughed, "Unlike you, Mr.

Bandit, I'm taking no chance of this wagon rolling over me."

"Just keep this thing on the road, so I don't have to get you out of another jam," Giuseppe retorted. "So, who do you think will make this masterpiece in marble?"

"No doubt, a man who fancies himself the next Michelangelo," Carlo said dreamily. "He was once one of us and paid us well."

"Yes," Giuseppe agreed, "But without us his David would have been stillborn!"

Transporting me over the road was the most expensive part. The more miles, the more money. The company paid a pittance to Carlo and Giuseppe for doing their harrowing work. The oxen team trudged slowly into Luna, their hooves striking cobblestones. No one looked up at me. They had seen so many carts flowing down the road from the quarry.

As they approached the harbor, Carlo and Giuseppe knew the most difficult part of the job was coming: hoisting me in a sling onto the ship. Even the great Michelangelo had been appalled when a sling broke. The slab snapped a sailor's neck. He was equally shocked to see his slab crash through the ship's deck and sink to the harbor bottom.

Thankfully, for Carlo and Giuseppe, the ship's crew was responsible for my next ordeal. After they hoisted me from the wagon, the oxen shook themselves, finally freed from my weight. Carlo turned the team around. His old friend Bandit dozed on the way back to the quarry.

PART THREE
JOURNEY

Mary Edmonia Lewis
Six to Nine Years Old
1851 - 1854

Before leaving Greenbush, my mother asked Father Clement to ride out to Samuel's school, to see if he would come with us to Niagara Falls. When he returned, and pulled back the flap to our wigwam, the sweat-soaked priest was alone. Our faces fell.

My uncle said, "You must be tired, Father."

Gathering up his dusty robe, the priest sat down and accepted a drink from a tin cup.

"Samuel wrote you this letter which I will try to read. Pardon my poor English"

My Beloved Half- Mother and Sister,

I am sorry but I must stay here at school. Now that I am a true orphan, I need to learn all I can to make a living. I need to speak perfect English, and learn my sums.

When I am done with school, I told you I would help you—especially you, my little Mary. My father told me the oldest son in Haiti should always help support his family.

I will visit you at Niagara Falls. Have someone write me a letter and tell me where you will be. I will find you.

If you want Mary to come to my school instead, they would be glad to take her here.

Sincerely,

Samuel

I watched Nimaamaa as the priest read the letter. Her eyes were shining with tears until Samuel's last sentence.

At that, my mother grabbed the letter from Father. "Mary will never go to one of those schools. They make our children wear white people's clothes and speak in white people's language. Mary is Ojibwe and always will be. Goodbye, Father, and thank you for all you have done."

❧

The next day we packed our things, took down our wigwams, and made ready to leave Greenbush. I stood still.

Nimaamaa commanded, "Come, Mary, hurry."

"I'm not going."

My mother knelt and gently put her hands on my shoulders. "I know you lost your father. But we are going to a place with the most beautiful trees and waters and animals that the Great Spirit has ever made."

I continued to sulk, until Nimaamaa added, "And maybe you can help me do my beadwork and sewing."

I smiled and said, "Really?" I never dreamed my mother would ask me to work with her in her high calling.

❧

We started for the Falls by following the path my aunts and uncles took to fish along the banks of the Hudson River. We must have made quite a sight to the few Dutch and French families living along the trail. The men carried our four birch bark canoes above their heads. Women and children dragged a platform of bark heaped with our belongings. Even our dogs helped out, with packs of supplies on their backs. My auntie wore a cradleboard on her back with my little cousin in it.

Although there were a few Mohawk and Iroquois families living near the Hudson, Indians were still an unusual sight. Sitting on their porches, the white people who knew us smiled and waved. Others stared.

When we got to the water, somehow we jammed everything we owned, including our dogs, into four canoes. That morning has always remained in my memory. The sun was shining; the water was still; the trees on either side of the Hudson held us in their lovely arms. It all seemed so perfect. Little did I know of what lay ahead!

Before we shoved off, Uncle Namyd scattered tobacco over the water. My imaamaa explained that it was to please any evil spirits in the river. If we made the Manitou happy, it probably would not trap us and pull us under.

"Probably" wasn't good enough for me.

Nevertheless, I began paddling hard. Even though I was slender and small, I was strong,

After half a day, my shoulders ached. Uncle Ogima had us pull our canoes to the riverbank, and gave us a little talk.

"We will soon reach the Erie Canal. There will be many canoes, but also a few big boats."

He told us these long boats carry cotton, or apples, or wood, and sometimes people. He added that there is a path above and that horses on the path pull the boats with ropes.

I couldn't imagine such a thing, but he went on.

"Then there are locks. We go in one side and a giant

door closes behind us. We hold onto ropes, as water rushes in, to keep our canoes steady. We wait until the water rises, and a giant door on the other side opens."

I figured it must have been a long time since Uncle Ogima had been on the canal, because when we got to the canal we could see there were many big boats and only a few canoes. The long boats looked like they could smash us to pieces.

Seeing how things had changed, Uncle Ogima set up a plan. The person in the middle seat of the last canoe would face the opposite way. Their job would be to yell, "Big boat!" when they saw one coming, so that we could paddle to the side of the canal.

One day, when I was the watcher, a big boat came towards us and seemed like it wanted to run us down. I yelled, "Big boat!" Everyone paddled hard but we just made it to safety. A guy on the big boat pumped a fist and yelled, "Get out of the way, you dirty Indians!"

"Don't listen to him, children," said my auntie. "We are a magnificent people!"

What was worse—being an Indian or a Negro? I asked myself.

The long boats were bad enough but the scariest part was going through the locks. For most of my life, I had lived in the quiet of nature. The worst sounds I had heard were horses pulling carts with squeaky wheels. That was nothing compared to the terrible screeching made by the opening of the first lock door. I clapped my hands over my ears.

When we were inside the lock, the water swirled so

much it was hard for my uncles to hold onto the ropes. I was terrified that our canoe would tip over. Thank goodness, the water calmed so we could escape our watery prison. The door opened at the other end of the lock and the hideous shrieking began again.

Oh, how I hated those locks, but I had to get used to them, because there were so many.

When I asked Uncle Ogima how long our journey would take, he said, "About 12 nights." That sounded like forever. He said that, when it got dark, we would camp along the canal. We would put our canoes over us if it rained. He assured us that we had plenty of dried food, but promised to hunt for fresh meat.

While he was saying this, dark clouds raced our way from the south. The air was still but we knew what was coming.

Uncle Namyd spoke up; "We must get off the canal, as soon as we see a good spot."

Then, out of nowhere, I felt the strong gust of wind that I first felt at Papa's burial. I thought it was from the approaching storm but no one else seemed to feel it. Could it be Baron Samedi protecting us on our journey?

"Are you hearing things again?" my mother asked.

"No," I lied. I didn't want anything to do with the spirit world.

Fortunately, we soon found a place with plenty of birch trees.

As we got out of our canoes, fat drops started to fall. After thanking the trees for their gift of shelter, my uncles stripped off their bark and stretched big strips from one canoe to another. We were going to sleep as though we were in a bark-covered grave.

Lightning tore through the night sky, screeched towards the earth, and lit up the forest around us. Abequa and I held hands under our covers.

I prayed to whatever spirit might listen: "Please make this stop!"

In the morning, there was no more rain. We pushed off the layers of bark and carried our canoes to the water. The sun shone brightly on the water.

My aunts and uncles chanted thanks to the Great Spirit and poured tobacco into the water again. Damp and bedraggled, we took off.

As the days passed by, we became tired of paddling and there was never enough to eat.

I finally complained, "Are we ever going to get there?"

No response.

I knew that my father would have comforted me, and maybe in his soft, singsong Haitian voice he would have told me some funny story about his village to get me laughing. He had only been gone a few weeks but I missed him so much.

Then one day we heard it. We turned to look where the sound was coming from.

Uncle Ogima put his hand to his ear. "I hear the Great Water God beating his drum." I paddled hard toward that sound.

When we got to the Falls, I was thunderstruck. All this time I had no idea what my family meant by "Thunder Waters," but one look at all that water rushing over the edge answered my question.

After admiring the Falls with reverence, my aunts and uncles took us to the spot where their band lived before they left for Greenbush. Amazingly, after seven years, there was still a group of about 50 Ojibwe living there. They greeted us with surprise.

The next day my uncles and other men in the band cut down tree saplings, bent them to form arches, and drove them into the ground. After they offered thanks to the birches, they stripped each one's bark in one piece and laid it over the arches. In one day, they built our new homes.

My mother and I put our things in one of the two wigwams, and that night after we pulled our deerskin blankets over us, she said, "I told you this was a good place."

I had to agree, and then I fell right to sleep.

After we settled in our new homes, my uncles suggested I come with them on a hunting trip. While they searched for deer, I used a slingshot to kill rabbits and squirrels. I learned to walk quietly in the woods to sneak up on the innocent little animals. I usually missed, but enjoyed the hide-and-seek.

When I wasn't hunting or playing with my cousins, I watched my mother as she sat sewing beads on cloth from the French traders, or on hides from my uncles' hunts.

One day I asked, "Nimaamaa, you said you would teach me to sew the beads. When?"

"Wait, Mary, while I finish this part."

Then she looked up. "Your little fingers may not work so well yet, but we'll try, tomorrow."

I felt that sudden wind again. I couldn't help but look startled, and Nimaamaa noticed. "It's the spirits again; I know you can feel them."

"No, I don't," I said, "I'm just excited about tomorrow."

"Maybe a spirit is telling you to take this journey with me."

"What journey?"

"Making pretty things to sell at the Falls, coming up with beautiful designs."

"Maybe."

"Listen to the spirit, Mary. It will guide you."

After hearing the wind again, I couldn't sleep that night. Auntie had put out the dream catcher for my little cousin. I heard him cry out. Auntie went to his side, rubbed his shoulders, and slowly waved the dream catcher over him. He fell back to sleep.

I didn't have any bad dreams that night; just wonderings about spirits, and excitement about working with my mother.

The next day, Nimaamaa had me sit outside with her, and began teaching me. She had a birch bark basket with all her supplies.

She showed me how to thread a needle and tie it at the end. She opened pouches; each contained a different color of beads. The sun was shining with full force and, as Nimaamaa opened each bag, the beads dazzled my eyes with their brightness.

My mother picked up one of the beads and held it up

for me to study. "These are called seed beads, because they are as tiny as seeds. If you want to learn how to do this, you have to stitch many, many of these beads onto cloth or deerskin. It's hard work. Are you sure you want to do this, Mary?"

I nodded.

Nimaamaa said, "You'll have to sit quietly for a long time. I know how you like to run around."

"I can play with my cousins any day. I want to make beautiful things."

Nimaamaa stared at me so hard it made me squirm.

"What?" I asked.

"You're close to the spirits, Mary," she said pulling me towards her. "Making beautiful things shows respect to the Great Spirit."

"Is that why Auntie made her cradleboard so fancy, with designs on the wood and all the pretty beadwork?"

"I'm glad you understand."

"And so my classes began. Whenever I designed and beaded and sewed, everything around me faded away, and I entered a new world.

∾⦾∾

The next two winters flew by as effortlessly as an eagle rides the wind above the rushing waters. I designed and sewed beadwork for moccasins, bandolier bags, and even pincushions. My designs and the quality of my work were crude, and my creations were not good enough yet to sell to the tourists. But Nimaamaa was patient.

She even taught me how to make little birch bark

boxes with quillwork. Nimaamaa called upon my uncles to get us small slabs of bark and quills left behind by porcupines. With those quills, Nimaamaa made brilliant fan and star patterns.

Aside from my work with my mother, I moved on to using a bow and arrow. Uncle Namyd made arrowheads for me by chipping stones. I helped care for the younger children, but also played in the forest and swam in a stream leading to the Falls. The roar of Thunder Waters was my constant companion.

I was nine winters old and mostly happy. But I had holes in my heart, losing my father and missing Samuel.

One summer day, as I was sitting on a blanket, sewing with my mother, a tall, skinny colored person came out of nowhere. Samuel?

I stood up and went to hug him, as did my mother. We were each on one side of Samuel, grabbing his hands, looking into his face.

"I got a break from school and, since I didn't have too much barbering, I thought I'd visit you."

Nimaamaa said, "My heart sings like a bird to see you."

I tried to match her. "My heart . . . my heart . . . shines like the sun to see you again."

Samuel patted my head. "Good one, Mary. Don't be getting too Ojibwe now; you're part Haitian."

I said, "Maybe I should thank Baron Samedi, then, for bringing you safely on your journey."

We all laughed.

In his black breeches, white shirt, suspenders, and beaked cloth cap, Samuel looked a little out of place with us, but in no time he mixed in with our group. He hunted and fished with the men during the day, and told us stories about his school and the places he worked in the evenings.

One night, as we sat around the fire, Nimaamaa asked him, "What are you going to do when you finish school? You can come live with us."

"I appreciate your invitation, Nimaamaa, but I have other plans. When I get out of school—in another year—I'm going to be a barber. Then I'll head out west where I heard people are discovering gold."

This was the first time he called our mother "Nimaamaa."

"Gold? What is so special about that old rock?" asked Uncle Ogima.

"Gold? People use pans to mine for it in streams. When they find gold, it brings lots of money."

"What do you want money for?" Uncle grumbled.

"I want to buy a house, have a family, a horse, and maybe some nice clothes."

"Do they have slaves out west?" The words just popped out of me.

"No!" said Samuel with certainty. "I'll pay for your education. You can get away from places that have slaves. Maybe even join me out west?"

Nimaamaa would have none of that. "She stays at home. No white man's school and, oh, Mary won't be going . . . out west."

Aunt Sarah chimed in. "We haven't told you this, Mary but we left the Credit Reserve north of here, where our parents live, because they live like white people: houses, farms, schools. We wore white man's clothes and they suggested we don't speak Ojibwe."

"I wouldn't want that. I like living in a wigwam," I said.

"I don't know if you will have much of a future." Samuel's eyes were serious. "If you don't learn to read and write."

Nimaamaa ended the discussion; "The future doesn't matter. We are happy now."

Samuel held his ground. "But, Nimaamaa, the world is changing. So many Ojibwe have been driven from the Falls. The white men cut down your trees to build houses and make you pay for your own land."

In a trembling voice, Uncle Ogima said, "We know that day may come, but we believe this land belongs to the Great Spirit. It cannot be sold."

"I know this is unfair," said Samuel as he leaned forward and touched my uncle's shoulder. "But it will come. And when it does, people will need jobs."

"Jobs!" my uncle snorted. "Hunting, skinning, cooking—aren't those our jobs?"

"I know you work hard, probably harder than any white person. But now people need a job that makes money, like a barber, or a teacher, or a minister."

Samuel looked at me. "Or someone who sells beautiful things. I don't know if you can make a living selling beadwork at the Falls, but people in cities do sculptures and paintings. Rich people pay big money for their work."

"We make enough from the tourists," Nimaamaa said firmly.

"Sure, enough to trade for pots and pans and cloth. I have nothing but respect for you, Nimaamaa. You took care of me even though you aren't my real mother. You and Mary were born with the talent to make beautiful designs."

Then Samuel's face broke into a smile. "Like I was born with ability to cut hair. I wonder, Uncle, could I cut off your braids? I could give you the latest haircut."

Samuel pretended to snip Uncle's braids and Uncle broke out a rare smile. By then the owls were hooting and the coyotes howling. So, we pulled our blankets around our shoulders and laid down. Nokomis put out the fire. I lay there full of thoughts about what Samuel had said.

We didn't have any further arguments with Samuel. We knew better than to ruin our remaining moments with him.

After Samuel left to go back to school, I didn't feel like playing with my cousins or hunting for rabbits. I only wanted to do my beadwork.

Then something terrible happened.

The Statue

DURING HER JOURNEY TO THE Falls, Mary suffered, but made it safely. And that's all that really counted to me. My journey to Roma was just as treacherous, if not more so, than Mary's.

When it began, men were loading me onto the sloop, the Bella Sposa. The ship was tied to the dock, with the magnificent harbor of La Spezia in the background. Three warships rode at anchor. Barges, merchant ships, and fishing boats darted around these battle cruisers, the pride of the Italian navy.

The harbor not only provided safety to its ships, it was the site of Italy's naval arsenal. Commissioned in 1861, it brought prosperity to La Spieza. The wealthy lived in villas with red-tiled roofs, spilling down to the sea.

Clearly visible in the distance was Mount Maggiore and the Apuan Alps. They appeared to be snow-covered, but it was really their marble faces, blinding white in the sun.

Captain Roberto Ferrara stood on the harbor side to oversee my loading. He was 55, with a deeply tanned face offset by graying black hair. He had a wife, Mariangelina, at home, and three grown children. He didn't see them for weeks at a time. He considered himself married to his ship, whose name, after all, meant "Beautiful Bride."

His senior officer, Vittorio Rossini, oversaw the 15-man crew. He had been an ambitious midshipman in the navy. But, unfortunately for him, Italy was at peace and commissions were scarce. Frustrated at being without a promotion or pay raise, Vittorio joined the crew of the Bella Sposa. He enforced military-style discipline on his ragtag crew of outcasts. Some were fleeing the law; others had escaped creditors, or the wrath of the women they had left behind.

Captain Ferrara gave a signal to Rossini to have me lowered into the hold. A group of crewmembers stood on deck to guide me, while others waited in the bowels of the ship to secure me. They gently lowered me through the dark opening to the bottom of the ship. Among the crew members waiting for me was Bettino Alinari, another refugee to the sea.

Bettino had grown up on a farm, tilling the rich soil of Tuscany. His family grew wheat, while their neighbors raised olives. The area was dotted with vineyards, and livestock roamed the pastures. Bettino saw only two problems with farming: it was boring and backbreaking. Oh, and there was a third one, a "papa" who was impossible to please.

I slowly settled on the bottom of the hold. There were two marble columns next to me, secured by heavy chains bolted to the hull. There were remnants of wheat and crushed olives on the floor. The ship had just carried a cargo from the Tuscan port of Livorno. The dock where they loaded it was where Bettino approached the captain and sheepishly asked for a spot on his ship.

Bettino's father had driven him to it. Every morning at 4:00 a.m. he was slapping the bottoms of his son's bare feet to wake him. Bettino couldn't see the need. They had no cows to milk. The wheat could wait. But his father couldn't stand "bodies in bed," as he said, and roused his only son to start his chores. Bettino's five sisters did needlework to generate income for the family, but didn't work in the fields.

Bettino and his shipmates pulled thick chains across me and made them tight. A slab sliding in a storm could sink a ship the size of the Bella Sposa. The weather was still clear, though, when they shut out the sunlight with the hatch cover. Bettino dreaded leaving the harbor. He had concealed this from the crew and captain, but the 18-year-old runaway suffered from seasickness.

In the darkness of the hold, I wasn't alone for long. Rats scampered across me, attracted by the stray wheat sheaves and crushed olives. The ship began to rise and fall on the swells of the Ligurian Sea as we headed south down the west coast of Italy to Rome's port of Ostia.

Above me, in the sailors' quarters, Bettino swung gently back and forth in his hammock, trying to keep his salt pork dinner down. As he focused on one of the oil lamps to steady his stomach, he reflected on how he had escaped his father's tyranny. He had wrapped his clothes in a blanket and pushed the bundle out the window. He clambered carefully to the ground. He did it silently, and no sounds came from the house. He left a note addressed to his little sister, Christina, as he imagined she would be the only one to cry.

Up in the captain's quarters, Captain Ferrara and Vittorio were enjoying a late-night card game. The sea was calm and the wind steady. Nonetheless, a lonely soul stood watch on deck, staring up at the stars. Ferrara slapped down a winning card and Vittorio stood up in disgust.

"Every time! How do you do it? If we were playing for money, I'd be your slave by now."

"That's a good suggestion, Vittorio, but who knows? Your luck could change."

"Luck has nothing to do with it," he retorted, "You need to change the deck. No doubt you've memorized the back of every card."

"Not just the backs, my son. You see the bent corner on this," flipping over the ace of diamonds. "And I spilled my coffee on this one," he said, holding up the king of clubs."

"Hah," Vittorio spat, "I knew no one could be that good."

"You shouldn't be complaining. You're lucky to have a captain like me. You have it soft here. We don't have cannons shooting at us. You must have been crazy to join the navy."

"It's these men that drive me crazy," Vittorio said. "At least in the navy I didn't have a crew of savages. They're lazy, and when I do give them a little work they get drunk and disappear at the next port of call. When I was serving on board—"

"Don't tell me about your war hero days—there was no war," Ferrara interrupted, lighting his pipe. "You were a peasant under the heel of those officers."

"No, what I mean, the men were decent. They wore uniforms, not filthy trousers. The ship didn't have wash hanging from the rigging. They called me, 'Sir,' not like these cutthroats."

"This isn't the navy, 'Admiral,' so stop pretending it is. And don't tell your captain he doesn't run an orderly ship." Ferrara yawned as he stood and patted the younger man on the shoulder. "If you show the men some mercy, I may let you win at cards someday."

The next morning we sailed into Ostia under a dazzling sun. The port city sat on both sides of the Tiber River, where it emptied into the sea. Bettino and his crewmates lounged at the rail. They held buckets and rags, but weren't using them. Rossini barked at them to climb the rigging to take down the large square sail.

Bettino and a crewmate opened the hatch, and sunlight sparkled on me. The sailors descended into the hold and unfastened my chains. They replaced these with ropes and raised me to the deck.

As Captain Ferrara guided the Bella Rosa into a slip, deckhands jumped off to tie her to the moorings. Bettino was one of them. He felt good standing on solid earth again, though his stomach still felt the motion of the ship.

A barge came alongside. Ten men drove it with their oars. They carefully lowered me. The barge was long and narrow, and my weight caused it to list to the port side, until they fastened ropes to resist my movement. The men strained against the oars as they covered the short distance from the Bella Sposa to the Tiber.

A team of oxen stood on the bank of the river. The men shipped their oars and then attached my barge to the team. One of the men led the sullen animals, while another walked behind, stinging their backs with his lash. I was only 60 kilometers from the Colosseum, but the journey could take weeks, depending on the strength of the current. The Tiber was at low water in the summer heat, but the oxen still had to fight it as they dragged me upstream to Roma.

PART FOUR
STARTING OUT

Mary Edmonia Lewis
1853 - 1857
Nine to Twelve Years Old

EXCEPT FOR THE DEATH OF my father, starting out in life was not too hard, but by the time I was nine, things changed. My mother suddenly became very ill. She couldn't hold anything down. My uncles built her a little birch bark wigwam. It was just too messy to keep her in ours. My aunties made her a soft bed and we all took turns staying by Nimaamaa's side.

We didn't know what was wrong with her, so we walked her to the wigwam of our band's medicine man. As we pulled back the flap, a dry old voice welcomed us.

We sat cross-legged, although my mother could hardly sit straight.

The medicine man asked us to be silent. He smoked some tobacco to purify the air and summon the Great Spirit.

After a few puffs, he said, "The spirits will tell me what kind of remedy I should give you." Swaying back and forth, he chanted, like Father Clement at Communion. His eyes became distant as he passed into another world.

Then he opened his medicine bag and took out some grassy material. Putting a small amount into my mother's hand, he said, "The spirits tell me this may work."

When she put it into her mouth, my mother made a face, but slowly chewed. She looked so miserable.

The medicine man did more chanting and said, "You may go now. The Great Spirit will heal you, if he so wills."

I was hoping for a miracle at that very moment, but that didn't happen. Within a few days, her skin turned bluish-gray.

I lay next to her—as I did almost all the time now—and Nimaamaa whispered to me that the Great Spirit was taking her to "the other side."

"No, he can't have you!" I cried.

Her breathing was rough. She fought for air.

"I'm sorry; first your papa, now me." She struggled to speak.

I clutched my mother's hand, and tears soaked my cheeks.

Breathlessly, she said, "Promise me, Mary."

I looked into her dimming eyes.

"Stay with our people . . ."

She began to go limp in my arms. "Stay at least three years on this side of the Falls . . . no slave catchers . . ."

She was barely breathing and her eyes froze in one spot.

"Don't go, Nimaamaa!" I sobbed.

But she did. Right before my broken-hearted, nine-year-old eyes.

In the days after my mother passed away, everything went by in a blur. But I remember we buried her in the Ojibwe way.

After the burial, we took our canoes north to the

Credit River Reservation to tell my grandparents they had lost their daughter.

When we pulled our canoes ashore, a tall man in a black suit walked toward us. He asked, "Are you lost?"

Aunt Elisabeth said, "Reverend Jones, don't you remember us?"

The man looked us over, "Yes—the John Mike family!"

Aunt Sarah smiled. "Yes, we left years ago for the Falls."

A serious look passed over the Reverend's face. "How is it at the Falls?"

Uncle Namyd reported that the fishing was good, and there were plenty of deer.

Reverend Jones tipped his hat. "I am glad it is still going well for you. I hope you will visit our chapel, while you're here. If not, a safe journey home."

As we walked up the road, Ojibwe people were working on small farms, going in and out of houses wearing white people's clothes. I asked Aunt Sarah, "Why do they live like this?"

"The reverend and his church thought we'd be better off learning the ways of the white people. They even got the government to give us money."

"Why didn't you stay here with Grandma and Grandpa?" I asked.

"Because we remembered living like real Ojibwe at the Falls."

"Your nimaamaa was only 16 but she wanted to come with us. Your grandparents didn't like it, but they let her go."

When we got to Grandma and Grandpa Mike's, they were glad to see us but a bit surprised. When we told them the reason for our visit, they were shocked. "How could this be? She was so young!"

My aunties put their arms around Grandma and Grandpa, and everyone cried. For the first time, I felt free to cry—not by myself but with my family.

That evening, we talked about life on the Credit Reserve.

"I thought I was getting away from trouble when I came to Canada," Grandpa Mike said. "But the council at our reserve treats me and my sons like we don't belong, because we're colored." I was struck by how dark his skin was, in contrast to his silver hair.

"We had so much hope when we came here," lamented my grandma, who was still wiping away tears from the death of her daughter.

Sheepishly, I said, "Grandma, may I ask you something? Are you colored?"

Grandma let out the closest thing to a laugh that we heard all day. "You noticed! My mother was Ojibwe and my father was colored, and I'm proud to be their daughter."

Just as I was starting to relax, my grandpa suddenly slammed his hand on the table. "Everywhere—Canada and the U.S.—we're treated bad because we're colored! We're not locked up in chains here, but . . ."

I looked down at my own brown hands.

"I wish I had some kind of a job," my grandpa said. "So we could leave here. I wish I could have learned to read and write."

Samuel's words came back to me.

When it was time to go, I was in such a fog from losing Nimaamaa that my family had to guide me to our canoes. I could not paddle.

Our canoes glided gently down the Credit River. At least the sun was bright on this sad day. I overheard Aunt Sarah saying to Aunt Elizabeth, "Seeing mother and father—it's painful."

When we arrived back at Thunder Waters, I wanted to retreat to my bed of pine boughs, but something fierce was brewing inside me. I walked a short distance from our wigwam, picked up a few pebbles, and threw them, one after another, against a big rock. Everything seemed so unfair.

Uncle Namyd gently grabbed my shoulders from behind.

I turned around and buried my head in his deerskin shirt. "The Great Spirit took my parents! I am an orphan now, like Samuel. Who will love me, take care of me?"

Uncle crouched down and met my eyes. "We will," he promised.

I cried some more. "Thank you, but it's still not the same."

"I know, but we will do our best."

With that, Uncle gently uncurled the fingers of my left hand and let the stones drop to the ground.

"That rock has a soul like you and me. It may be sad or even mad that you tried to hurt him."

That spirit stuff again!

"Tell the rock you're sorry. Then, ask if you can draw on him someday. It is good to tell your story on a rock, when you're sad, or maybe after a dream. The rock listens. Everything else dies. Trees die. Your nimaamaa's purses will fall apart. But a rock lives forever."

I held Uncle Namyd's hand, looked at the rock, and silently asked it to forgive me. I had no idea how important stone would be to me some day.

Over time, I became my old self again, but not before suffering a terrible nightmare. It came in the middle of winter. Every year, when the cold winds of November came, we moved away from the river and built wigwams further inland, where it was warmer. My uncles snow-shoed back and forth to the river to hunt beaver. Beaver pelts were the thickest when it was cold, and they sold them to traders in the spring. Europeans liked beaver fur for their hats. Meanwhile, we lived mainly on dried meat from the summer hunts. When it snowed hard, we stayed in our wigwams night and day.

My family didn't mind being shut in. Frigid days and nights were the time for stories, and my family had lots of them. My Uncle Ogima told us how when he was a boy he took his canoe out in stormy weather. The canoe turned over, and he could swear an evil Manitou was pulling him down.

My cousins and I cringed.

Seeing our fear, Uncle Namyd said in a comforting way, "Ogima, it was just seaweed."

I couldn't sleep that night. It was snowing hard, and a wicked wind was shaking our wigwam. Although we had deerskin coverings and trade blankets, we huddled together for warmth.

Finally, sleep descended. I dreamed of an old woman sitting on the ground where we sold souvenirs. Her clothes were full of dust, as if she was part of the earth. She wore a wide skirt, and on her lap she held a frayed, old bandolier bag, and a pair of filthy moccasins. She called out to passing tourists, "Handmade souvenirs!" People paid no attention, so she begged, "Can you spare a penny? Anything?"

When I got closer to her in my dream, I saw her face—it was me!

I sat up and screamed.

Auntie quickly took the dream catcher from my little cousin and dangled it over my head. Nestled next to me, my cousin Abequa said, "Don't be afraid, you just had a bad dream."

Auntie stroked my hair and said, "It's nothing, Child. Go back to sleep."

The next morning, I realized what my dream meant. Without a job—like Samuel said—without a trade, I would be that woman. I kept this in my heart and shared it with my rock when I got the chance.

I drifted through the winter. On better days, gliding across the snow in snowshoes. On the blustery ones, sleeping, playing inside games with my cousins, and listening to my family's stories. I found myself doing mean things, like throwing over a game board when I was losing, and ignoring my uncles when they told their silly stories. They gave me stern looks but said nothing.

When spring came, I awoke screaming in the middle of the night. An ugly Manitou with big teeth and a large blue head was chasing me. Drowsily, Abequa clasped my hand, and Aunt Sarah murmured it was time for me to have my own dream catcher.

In the morning, I went outside and found my Aunt Sarah had gathered some twigs, rocks, beads, and deer sinew.

I sat down next to her. "Is that for my dream catcher, Auntie?"

"Yes. It'll get rid of the bad dreams. Only the good ones will get in.

She paused and then added, "This will help you sleep. Then she looked sternly at me. "And maybe make you a nicer girl."

I knew I had that coming.

Aunt Sarah abruptly changed the subject. "Why don't you get your mother's basket and make souvenirs for the tourists again? It might be good for you."

I needed that, a hard job to take my mind off my losses. But when I entered the wigwam and saw Nimaamaa's basket, it was too much. How many times had my mother used that basket? How could I handle her needles, cloth, beads, and thread?

Then, suddenly, a white hand hovered over the basket, bringing cool air. It just sat there, hovering. With all the courage I could muster, I moved my hand to touch the hand. It flinched, fled, and left a filmy trail.

"Jibay! (Ghost!)" I yelled. The hand took the cold with it, but my teeth chattered.

Auntie called, "What's wrong?"

"Nothing, Auntie. I'll be right out," I stammered. I didn't want anyone knowing about these strange things.

Although I didn't want to touch my mother's basket, I made myself do it. I picked it up and brought it outside.

I walked into the forest to my rock. The sudden winds, the ghostly hand. Am I going crazy?

I remembered what Uncle had said about drawing on the rock. I found a stone with a sharp edge. As much as the hard rock would allow it, I traced my fingers to make a simple picture of a hand.

When I finished, I strolled back to Aunt Sarah.

Now I felt ready to make beautiful things, as my nimaamaa had.

Aunt Sarah and I worked side by side in silence. She made me a lovely dream catcher!

I made a design for a bandolier bag. I cut out a pattern for moccasins. On the bag and the moccasins, I spelled out "Niagara Falls" in beads. Our priest had shown me how to write those two words and I felt so proud.

Priests like him made me want to go back to the church in Greenbush. The ways of the church and Ojibwe people were almost the same. The priest spoke of the Holy Spirit and angels; our Ojibwe spoke to spirits. The priest purified the air with incense; the medicine man smoked tobacco. The priest chanted in a language I didn't understand; the medicine man did the same.

But I was most drawn to the Catholics' Jesus. Maybe this had something to do with a life-size statue of Jesus back in our church in Greenbush. Jesus seemed more real than the invisible Ojibwe spirits. And the priest said we could turn to him with our problems.

I certainly had problems as the years passed. Without Nimaamaa and Papa, loneliness was my constant companion. Because I was part colored, fear was not far behind. I wasn't a baby anymore, and now that I was starting out in life, I felt like a misfit.

Anger spewed out of me as regularly as the Niagara River spilled over the edge of the Falls. Searching for some comfort, I asked if I could go to the Catholic Church. My aunt and uncle seemed happy to get rid of me.

Every Sunday I attended Mass. The building was small, but large enough for the French traders and a few of us Ojibwe.

❦

Eventually, I felt well enough to return to Goat Island with my aunties, where we sold our souvenirs. I had learned to count money and make simple change. But I had absorbed something far more important that would serve me well: I had learned how to sell.

People who came as tourists to the Falls were fascinated by us. They stared at our clothing and braided hair. They watched as we sewed and beaded.

They commented on my work in particular.

"You are young to be doing such gorgeous work," they would say.

Sometimes, if I was with my auntie, they asked if she was my mother.

"No, her mother passed away."

Their faces turned sorrowful. They would ask to see what I made, and purchase my goods.

One day Aunt Sarah and I laughed after a day of selling and watching the tourists with their pitiful looks. We agreed that having her with me would help our sales. My auntie would tell customers how my mother passed away. The person would feel sorry for me, comment on my "talent," and buy whatever I was selling.

So, I learned how to play on people's feelings to get them to buy.

When I was about 11, the priest came to read us a letter from Samuel. Samuel had contacted a man named Captain S.R. Mills, who, with his wife, held a little school in their house. In his letter, Samuel sent money and asked my family to bring me to the Mills' home for lessons.

Not much excited me during this period in my life. I plodded along with Aunt Sarah as she led me through the forest to the Mills' home. It was a little, white-painted house with a porch. This was the first time I had set foot in a house with curtains, fancy papered designs on the walls, tables, and kerosene lamps.

One day, when my auntie walked me to school, I told her about the plates with knives, forks, and spoons that we used for our lunches at the Mills'.

Auntie scowled. "Oh, you like them better than your wooden bowl and spoon?"

"I didn't mean it that way. Anyhow, don't tell them, but I think the captain and his wife look funny."

"Why?"

"They are all white, pink, and plump, and have hardly any hair."

"They are old, Mary."

"I know, but their faces and their hands are so pink. People make fun of us for being colored, but I think we look better than them."

For once, we shared a good laugh.

I was in a class with three French boys who knew no English. Since I could speak and understand some English, I was a step ahead of them. I liked the classes. Just as enjoyable as learning my letters was getting into mischief whenever Captain Mills turned his head. The boys and I made faces behind the old man's back. When he was teaching, we quietly kicked each other under the tables. This little school helped me get back something I thought I had lost forever—my giggle.

Then one day I realized I had kept my promise to my mother; I had remained with my family for three winters after losing Nimaamaa. I really hadn't planned on doing anything but remaining with my band—until my brother Samuel came back.

Cleopatra

MY START IN LIFE WAS a lot different from Mary's.

Alexandria—the Romans were huddling in caves when we built this magnificent seaport with its vast harbor. A towering lighthouse guided merchant ships to our shores. Our powerful fleet protected us against invasion. Our temples and palaces dwarfed the Roman villas. We were performing surgeries while they were still inking their skin. In fact, medicine became my favorite subject.

Not that I was always studious. No one lived to breathe the desert air and feel its heat more than me. I loved nothing more than mounting my beloved Alixir and galloping across the sands. His untamed spirit frightened some, but, with me, he was playful as a puppy.

I was trotting back to my palace one morning, after riding my horse hard. There was a sheen to his coat and foam coming from his mouth. As I handed the reins to a servant, Alixir gently nuzzled me. I was ten years old and proud to be the daughter of a king. One day I might sit on his throne. I pranced into the palace wearing my white dress.

I twirled and spun, as my brothers and sisters pretended to read their lessons. "Aren't we the precious one," my older sister, Berenike, snarled. "We're trying to study, and your ugly face is a distraction."

Her mother had been Greek, and Berenike's complexion was as white and smooth as porcelain. She avoided the desert sun, lest it spoil perfection. Her lustrous hair framed her exquisite features. She had adorable dimples, of course, and deep-set dark eyes in perfect proportion to her lovely nose.

But there was nothing lovely about her harsh tone and accusing eyes.

"Study?" I retorted. "Since when have any of you listened to the teachers father gave us? When was the last time you visited the library? Have you ever even been inside our medical school?" I was referring to my two favorite haunts. One was the greatest library the world had ever known; the other, called the Mouseion, was the world's first center for medical research. I would later write my own book on disease.

Berenike had had enough with my insolence. Furious, she grabbed my hair and pulled me to the floor. I was on my back on the cold marble. She sat atop me, knowing that my worst nightmare was to be restrained. I struggled as she stretched my straining arms and kneeled on my biceps. I was helpless. "Tell me again about your peasant mother, who gave you this ugly face."

"This is not my mother's face! Don't you recognize your father in my eyes?" I said this through clenched teeth, as I fought to get her off.

The servants pretended not to notice. The musicians kept up their steady play. A barefoot servant glided across the marble bearing a golden plate of fresh figs. She had a taster in tow to make sure they were not tainted. Poisoning was a leading cause of death in my family.

Tired of tormenting me, hungry for figs, Berenike climbed off my arms. My little brothers, both named for their father, grabbed the figs greedily. My little sister, Arsinoe, waited until the taster had remained upright a sufficient time, before eating one. I rubbed circulation back into my arms. Berenike had her mouth full but she wasn't through with me.

Pointing at my white gown, she scoffed, "Who are you today? Venus in the flesh?"

I frowned—a Roman god. "No, I am who I always

have been: the daughter of Isis. Someday, I will be worshipped as Isis."

Berenike recoiled at my blasphemy. "So, our Greek gods are not good enough," she cried, pointing at the statues that stood about the room. "You embrace the religion of these peasants, along with their savage language."

My sister knew all the places she could hurt me, inside and out. Insulting my love for languages! My desire to speak to my people.

My chin trembled. I didn't want to give her the satisfaction of seeing my tears but I couldn't hold back. I ran from the room, sobbing, to the one person who could always heal my wounds.

I ran through massive columned rooms, past the giant image of the Sphynx. Guards in doorways moved aside for me as they bowed. I pushed open heavy ornate doors and startled servants waving white feathered fans. I passed through rooms and interrupted poets in mid-verse. I bounded up the grand staircase and rushed into my father's chamber.

My father was reclined on a couch, conferring with his advisors about the sad state of the treasury. When he saw my red face, he dismissed them. He sat up to face me and took my hands.

"Let me guess, it's your big sister again."

I buried my face in his robe. "Who does she think she is?" I wailed. "She carries herself like a queen and treats me like a beggar."

He stood me up and looked at me with hard eyes. "Cleopatra, you must promise me to be careful around your brothers and sisters. As you know, there has been much blood spilled in our family, for the sake of this throne." I had heard the stories of aunts poisoning their husbands, even mothers murdering their children. Blood meant nothing to my family, unless it was royal.

He continued in his stern manner. "Berenike is very ambitious. After I'm gone, she'll do anything to seize power."

"Oh, don't talk like that," I said lightly, "You are a god. You will never die."

He remained stern and said in a scolding tone. "I've heard that you ride a horse like a man. You hunt like a man. My subjects think you're not my daughter." He became agitated. "You're supposed to be a princess!"

I answered him simply; "If they think I'm man or woman, I don't care. As long as they believe I'm their god."

He smiled and stood up. "My goddess—that's above princess—it's good you came to see me today." He reached behind the couch and brought up a shiny object.

I gasped. It was a statue of Alixir at full gallop, every detail correct, every muscle captured, and cast in solid gold. "Oh, father," I said, my heart full, "It's gorgeous." I reached for it. "Be careful, your horse is very heavy," he said, as he handed it to me. Despite his warning, I almost dropped it. Then I clutched Alixir to my chest. I couldn't wait to show it to Berenike and watch the jealousy creep into her eyes.

PART FIVE
EVOLUTION

Mary Edmonia Lewis
Twelve to Fourteen Years Old
1855 - 1858

WHEN I FIRST SAW SAMUEL, I couldn't believe it was him. He was taller than my uncles, and his muscles bulged where his short-sleeved shirt stopped. But he still had that twinkle in his eye that told me he viewed life as a great adventure.

He had first looked for me at our wigwam, but Nokomis had told him I was selling souvenirs down at Goat Island. It had been three years and many a nightmare since I'd seen Samuel.

When we first met, we were speechless. He was indeed a man, and I was a full 12 years old.

"You're so tall," I said. He didn't say the same to me, because I was short for my age.

"Where were you all this time?" I demanded.

"After I finished school, I stayed in a boarding house in Albany for a few years. I was barbering and playing the banjo to make money for my trip out west."

"And now you are leaving," I said, bitterly.

"Yes, but first I have something to do."

"What?"

"I'm taking you to school, Mary Edmonia Lewis."

"Hmph." No one had called me by my full name since Papa used it when he was mad. Samuel chuckled, but I was still angry. "You made my family take me for English classes last year without asking me."

"I wanted you be able to read the words if I sent you a letter."

I softened my tone, "I did like the school, though."

"Wonderful." Samuel paused and then continued, "I told you how the oldest Haitian brother takes care of his younger sisters and brothers." His voice became tight. "You are all I have, and I am all you have. I will take care of you, but there's no future selling trinkets to tourists."

"You said that before," I said, acting as if I was bored.

"You could become an artist, a teacher, or a lawyer. You're smart for your age. You can be someone important someday, like I will be."

As we talked, a tourist asked the price of a pair of moccasins. I answered with my usual sales smile. The woman muttered, "Pretty, but too much," and walked away. My childlike charm no longer worked.

If only shoppers knew how much time I spent making these things. I looked up at Samuel and said, "I can quit selling for today. Let's go home. Everyone will want to see you."

Over the next few days, Samuel explained as much as he could about the new school. He finally convinced me to try it. We would have to travel quite a distance to New York Central College in McGrawville. Samuel told my doubtful aunts and uncles that this was not a school to change Ojibwe children. Rather, it was a religious school, where they wanted to do away with prejudice. It was one of the few schools that accepted girls, as well as coloreds and Indians.

"It has three important Negro professors! This school

will prepare Mary for a job. There is no future for her here. Mary and the rest of you, if you stay at the Falls, someday the last Ojibwe family will be ordered to leave."

My usually calm Uncle Namyd tossed a big stick into the fire and flames flew up. Nokomis gave him an angry look and rearranged the embers.

"Mary is my little sister. I have to watch out for her," Samuel said.

Everyone was silent.

"Anyhow, she has more obstacles to overcome than the rest of you."

Samuel was full of these fancy words.

"I'm sorry, Mary, but you will always be treated as a lesser person unless you get a job that brings you respect."

Aunt Sarah muttered, "That's what Father said."

Finally, Uncle Ogima said, "We will let her go to that school."

"I'll take her there," Samuel said. "We'll take a line boat to Syracuse, then a train to McGrawville."

"When we get there, will you stay with me for a while?" I begged.

"No, I can't," Samuel said. "After I drop you off, I'm heading west." Seeing my face drop, he added, "I'm sure you'll make friends quickly."

Frowning, I fingered my rabbit fur pillow.

"Don't worry, Mary. We'll write to each other."

Before we left the Falls, I talked to my big rock. "I'm leaving with Samuel, but I'll be back. Thanks for always listening."

With that, I took out a sharp stone I kept in my pouch

and carved a road ending with a book. A simple drawing, but my rock was too hard for anything more difficult.

And then I felt and heard it again! A single gust of wind that flew my way and made the fallen autumn leaves dance round and round. This time I was startled but not terrified. Perhaps—just perhaps—it was a spirit that would bring me safely through my next journey!

This time we traveled by line boat. It felt safer on the line boat than in our canoes, but when we went through the locks I still hated the screeching. There were a few canoes. I felt sorry for the paddlers, and gave them a friendly wave.

Our boat carried what my brother called "lumber." I called them "murdered trees."

Since the trees came from land along the Niagara River, I wondered where they had cut them down. Would my family's forest home be next?

I said to Samuel, "I bet they never even asked the trees for forgiveness."

"What?" he asked, with a puzzled look.

"Never mind," I said. Samuel was not brought up as an Indian; he wouldn't understand.

Questions ran through my head. What would this new school be like? Would I get along with the other students? Were the teachers mean?

I was thankful when we got to Syracuse and came ashore from the boat with the dead trees. Samuel checked us in at a hotel where he said we could get washed up and rest before going to McGrawville.

"You know, Mary, no hotel would take us down South."

I was about to ask why, and then I remembered. I would always have to remember.

Samuel explained what it would be like to take a train, but when the noisy steel machine arrived in a cloud of smoke, I backed away.

Samuel smiled at my reaction. He took my hand and gently led me up the stairs.

When we got to our car, I saw rows of seats on both sides. We were the only coloreds. Samuel spotted a bench toward the rear. As we walked down the aisle, I bumped an elderly white woman whose foot was dangling into the aisle. She grunted, pulled her foot back, and looked at me as if I had attacked her.

When we arrived in McGrawville, Samuel searched for a carriage to take to my new school. I couldn't help but comment, "That lady looked so mad. I only tapped her."

"There are still a lot of ignorant people around here. But if you come out west with me, you won't have to put up with it."

Then my brother spotted a horse and carriage nearby, with a sign reading, "New York Central Pick-Up."

The driver welcomed us. "Are you one of the new girls?"

"Yes," I said, meekly, not knowing what to expect from white people.

Samuel whispered. "Say, 'Yes, sir.'" And I added the "sir."

"Every September I look forward to meeting the new

students. School started last week, but there's always a few stragglers like you." He turned and smiled like he didn't want to give offense.

The horses' hooves hit the road with a beat as regular as my uncles' drums. The driver turned onto a path that passed over a creek. Then the driver extended his arm and said, "There's your school."

THE OLD NEW YORK CENTRAL COLLEGE AT MCGRAWVILLE, N. Y.

Several buildings spread across a large piece of rolling land.

"It's big!" I exclaimed.

Samuel put his arm around my shoulder, pulled me close, and smiled with pride over the fine school he had chosen.

I was thrilled myself, and hoped I would fit in.

Cleopatra

MY FATHER HAD BEEN RIGHT about my sister, Berenike. While he was away in Rome, begging for a loan to replenish the treasury, my older sister showed her ruthlessness by seizing his throne. Berenike was almost a woman now and she had the support of the richest and most powerful in Alexandria.

When word reached Rome about Berenike, it wasn't just my father who was outraged. Having lent large sums to him, the Romans now had a financial interest in restoring my father to power. They dispatched an army to invade Egypt. Among the soldiers was a dashing cavalry commander, Marc Antony.

The Romans crossed into Egypt and fought two fierce battles against Berenike's forces. My father was so angry at her betrayal he wanted to slaughter his disloyal subjects, but Antony stayed his hand.

At last, the Romans reached Alexandria and overran the palace. I was huddling with my brothers and little sister in our private quarters. Outside, we could hear the clang of metal and shrieks of pain. To calm my brothers and sister, we played "school," and I was their teacher. They barely paid attention, their eyes wide and filled with fear.

There was a pounding on our door, as someone demanded we open it. I crept to the door and asked who was there. "Antony. Your father wants to see you immediately." I was only 14, a mere slip of a girl. My skin had spots and my hair was unruly. I didn't want to see anybody, least of all a Roman soldier.

Antony tried a gentler tone; "Come on, Princess, your father misses you. He spoke only of you during our long journey." Arsinoe helped me lift the heavy bar and together we pushed open the thick door. Standing before us, with a bemused look, was a tall, strapping man. He had dark, curly hair and kind eyes. He wore a golden breastplate and a flowing red tunic. I couldn't help noticing his sword was streaked with the same red color.

Seeing my embarrassment, he bowed slightly. "Ah, the famous Cleopatra. Your father told me you were the 'son' he always wanted." He looked me up and down. "Now I know what he means," he said, with a sly grin. If I could have reached his face, I would have slapped it. He moved past me and scooped up the cowering boys. "Come on, we're all going to see your baba."

I loathed this insolent man but had no choice but to follow him to my father's chamber. There were signs of battle everywhere; broken furniture, the floor stained red, smoke rising in the distance. There were still some muffled cries as the Romans finished executing the wounded. I didn't know then that Berenike had also been put to the sword.

When my father saw us, he extended his arms. He wasn't the same man who had left months before. He was thin and his hands trembled. There were deep creases in his forehead and his eyes looked hollow. He had lost his royal bearing and his shoulders slumped like the Roman subject he had become. Nevertheless, I was overjoyed to feel his warm embrace again.

"Baba," I whispered. No more words came. He lifted my chin.

"You are too old to call me that. Your sister is gone. You must take her place."

I was shocked to hear of Berenike's death, but

inwardly pleased she had gotten what she had deserved. My brothers and sister wrapped around my father's legs. He looked down at them, amused.

He only spoke to me. "You must be a woman now. The time for riding horses is over." No matter how sternly he spoke, I could still see a slight sparkle behind his eyes.

"Alixir died while you were gone," I told him, haltingly. "We were out for a ride. Oh, Baba, there was a loud crack and he collapsed in pain." My tears flowed from the memory.

He stood me up and held my shoulders. "It's just as well. I forbid you to do any more riding. You will be carried on a throne."

"I wanted Alixir to have his own pyramid," I rushed on. "But Berenike—she had him buried in the sand like a common creature."

"Cleopatra, that's enough. We have serious matters to discuss." He commanded his servants to remove my brothers and sister from the chamber. He had me sit opposite him at his ceremonial desk. He held up a piece of writing.

"This is my will," he said, gravely. "When I am gone, I'm leaving my kingdom to you and your younger brother Ptolemy."

I was aghast at such talk. "You come back to us after all this time, to talk of death?"

He told me to hush. "You will follow our family's tradition and marry your brother."

I was revolted. One of the reasons the Romans

considered us savages was that we intermarried to preserve our precious bloodlines.

Seeing my disgust, my father slightly softened his tone. "It won't be a marriage like the one me and your mother had. It's strictly a royal arrangement. You and Ptolemy can find love elsewhere. Don't forget you will both be gods."

There was just too much to take in. "That is my dream, Father, but I don't want it, if it means losing you."

I came around the desk and hugged him from behind. He pried my hands away and turned to face me.

"You must be strong. And, I warn you again, be careful. Berenike may be gone, but when your brothers and sister come of age, they will be just as dangerous."

I smiled. I couldn't imagine those brats becoming a threat. "Don't worry, Father. But please eat something."

He sighed and looked down at his trembling hand that still held his will. "Call my servant. We must have a feast!"

Despite his heavy debts and cruel creditors, my father resumed his lavish spending. He restored the grandeur of our palace and continued to spoil us with costly gifts.

After the Romans restored my father to the throne, we thought they would leave, but they humiliated us by leaving a garrison to protect their investment. The Roman soldiers had their way with Egyptian women, royal and common. A new strain of children appeared in the streets of Alexandria, adding another voice to the cacophony of languages.

The Romans had gradually conquered the lands of our empire and now they had conquered us. Antony was a frequent visitor to our palace, as he was a favorite of my father. They drank late into the evenings, while Antony regaled him with boasts of his bravery in legendary battles. One day, I was practicing my Latin aloud, when Antony must have overheard.

He walked into my room, wearing his splendid uniform, as usual. "Ah, you're finally learning a civilized language," he said, in his usual mocking tone.

"I don't see much choice," I said, sulkily. "Soon the whole world will have to learn."

"Cleopatra, you have us wrong. We do not impose our language and customs on the people. We just plunder their wealth, enslave their men and . . ." he trailed off.

"I know what you do to our women," I said, glaring at him.

"Don't worry, Princess," he said, in his condescending way. "We will not allow any harm to come to the daughter of Isis."

I stood facing him. "Why are you bothering me?"

He suddenly looked serious. "Because I've been under your spell since that day you unlocked your door."

I flushed in embarrassment. No one had dared to address me in such familiar fashion.

"You're an old man," I said, haughtily. "Besides, didn't you say I looked like a boy."

"It's true, Cleopatra," he said, evenly. "I am twice your age. But, I want you to know it's not your looks that have bewitched me."

I was startled, but tried to keep my face from showing it. "Oh," I asked, off-handedly, "So, what is it that attracts you?"

Antony reached for my hands but I didn't give them. "It's your fine intelligence. You're the smartest woman I have ever met. You have an indomitable spirit. Though you're still a child, I can speak to you like you're a woman."

"I'm going to marry my brother, so you can forget any dreams. The thought of marrying a Roman—it disgusts me."

I was surprised to see the hurt in his eyes.

He lowered his voice. "Cleopatra, you are young, but someday you might discover this old man has something to offer. Your father knows me well—a man of character."

I was tired of his nonsense, but his flattery had touched me. I also couldn't help feeling sorry for him; he was so far from home.

"I will always be grateful for what you did for my father," I said, removing the edge from my voice. "But there is no future. Even if I rule this land someday, I will just be another subject of Rome."

"No, Cleopatra," he said, impulsively grabbing my hands. "There is not another woman on Earth with your brilliance. They even know about you in Rome, thanks to your father. There will be a day when every Roman citizen knows your name."

"Thank you," I said, softly, looking down, while my hands went to my side. "No one has ever spoken to me like this. I like it—for you—to see me as I am, not just how I look." I continued cautiously, "I'm beginning to think you're more intelligent than you look. Perhaps we can talk from time to time? I have so many subjects I'm interested in but no one to share them with."

He smiled. It looked sincere for a change. "There is nothing I would desire more, Princess. Unfortunately, I've been recalled to Rome. I sail tomorrow. You will always be in my heart. I pray that our paths cross once more. But, next time, I will not come as your conqueror, but as your friend."

I didn't believe a word, but returned the smile. "Perhaps by then, my harsh tongue will have softened. I will speak like a queen, not an impudent child."

"May I embrace you, Princess, before I go?" he asked, shyly.

I tried to keep my back arched but he pressed me close. "I will always protect you, Cleopatra. Just wait, I will send for you one day."

I couldn't suppress a giggle. No one "sends for" the daughter of Isis.

Mary Edmonia Lewis

How can I describe my time at New York Central? It was good to be with children my age. And I wanted to learn to read and write. I appreciated how the teachers helped me speak better English. But I couldn't handle the ways they had of doing things, and it seemed they couldn't handle me.

My first surprise was the loud, strange sound I heard after my brother and I finished our talk with the head mistress. Miss McKagg had looked at me with kind eyes and asked me questions. I was too shy to speak but Samuel filled her in on everything.

Miss McKagg explained, "All we want of our students

is that they be of good character and be willing to learn. We wish to give everyone this opportunity, especially the colored children."

At the word "Colored," she looked at me and smiled. Little did she know I saw myself as mainly Ojibwe. And I didn't want to be thought of as "special."

"Why is this school called a college when you even take 12-year-olds like Mary?" Samuel asked.

"The younger students go to preparatory school. The classes prepare them for the more advanced courses in the college."

Just as she said that, there was a loud clanging. I almost jumped from my chair.

"Those are just the classroom bells," Miss McKagg said, soothingly.

Wanting to fit in, I simply said, Oh, I knew that."

"What goes on here will be new to you. You're used to life in the wild, but we will help you." We walked out in the hall. Boys and girls were bursting out of doorways, all speeding in the same direction. Behind them strolled bearded young men and their female classmates—they must have been college students.

Everything at the school was based on bells. They rang when it was time to wake up, eat, go to class, and go to bed. It was completely unlike life at Thunder Waters, where we got things done in a natural way, with the sun as our clock.

On that first day, Miss McKagg took me to the dining room and had me sit with other children on a bench at a long table. All these people eating and talking at one time—I wasn't used to this. I was thankful they had given me forks, knives, and spoons at the Mills' school, because I knew how to handle them. A woman in an apron brought me a plate of food I had never seen or smelled before. My stomach turned over.

Then there were the clothes: white blouses with aprons or pinafores down to our ankles, heavy leather shoes. How I longed for my soft buckskin dresses, leggings, and high-topped moccasins.

Another problem was "Chapel"—daily services with singing, praying, and long speeches, much of it for the college students. This involved so many big words I could hardly stay awake. The only speaker who stirred me was a colored man, Frederick Douglass. We had just learned about volcanoes in geography. The way he spoke, it was like a volcano erupting. He talked of slavery: how colored, Indian and white people should be equal. He also wanted men and women to be equal. When he said, "Abolition," it was new to me; otherwise I understood every word.

But one great speech by Frederick Douglass was not enough for me to like Chapel. I longed for our Jesuit church, where I didn't have to just listen. I could actually do things, like make the sign of the cross, kneel, and receive Communion.

I had three roommates at my new school. We slept in bunk beds. One night, I was lying awake in the darkness. I didn't want to wake my roommates but couldn't hold back my tears. On the top bunk across from me, Priscilla whispered, "What's wrong? If you miss your parents, we all do." Little did she know how much I missed mine. I didn't want anyone to know I'd lost my parents. It was fine to be an orphan when my aunties and I worked on customers' sympathy, but now that I was 12, I just wanted to be like everyone else.

I said, "I miss my buckskin dress, my soft moccasins, my family's rabbit stew."

"Are you an Injun?" Priscilla asked, matter-of-factly.

"Some call us that."

"Do you have any of your Injun stuff with you?"

"I do, but please call me Ojibwe or Indian."

Priscilla became excited. "Take your Indian stuff out tomorrow, during naptime? You can show us your 'O–jib-we' things," she painfully pronounced.

I smiled in the dark. "That would be . . . fun."

The next day, when the obnoxious bell clanged at three o'clock, we headed to our rooms for a nap. Priscilla whispered to our two roommates that we were going to play Indian. They giggled and said they wanted to join us. Out of a drawer, I pulled a blanket where I had wrapped my deerskin tunic and breeches, along with a beaded necklace and a pouch filled with herbs that our medicine man gave me in case I got sick.

My colored roommate, Ida, asked to wear the necklace, and my two white roommates, Priscilla and Ella, each tried on my deerskin clothing.

"Make up a story, Mary, and we'll act out the parts," Ida suggested.

We put a blanket over our heads, and I had the girls pretend that a wicked Manitou was out to get us. Only my medicine could save us. I took out a few tiny grass-like pieces from my pouch and tossed them in the air. They sprinkled down on us inside our little pretend wigwam.

"The Manitou—it sounds like a ghost," declared Ella.

"What's that?" I asked.

Ida said, "It's usually white and . . . you can see through it. They say it's a dead person who's come back."

"Oh, our word for that is Jiibay." I thought of the white hand hovering over my mother's sewing basket. The memory sent a shiver through my body.

In the days ahead, we kept sneaking moments to play Indian. I got braver and began kidding around with girls from other rooms. I pretended my medicine pouch held miracle cures.

I made up a story, which I pretended was true, that my Ojibwe family gave me the name "Wildfire," because I was so full of energy, and my brother Samuel the name "Sunrise," because he was so bright and warm.

I told them my uncles went into the woods and fasted until a spirit whispered these names to them. They gave the names to us at a ceremony.

Actually, my family didn't follow these traditions any more. We believed the arrival of white settlers and tourists had caused most of the spirits to leave. But I made up this story, along with others, because I loved the way the girls giggled. It made me feel special.

I was making friends but wasn't having the same success at my lessons. I liked drawing class and I didn't mind arithmetic, but literature and moral philosophy—I hardly understood a word.

I couldn't pronounce a lot of English words. People

often couldn't undertand me, because I ran words together the way we Ojibwe did. I hated repeating myself. My teachers stayed after class to help me with my English, but Miss McKagg, our headmistress, helped me the most.

Another problem was that I couldn't sit still for long. I was used to doing, not listening. That's why I did well in drawing class, where I could actually do something.

One day, Miss McKagg came to my moral philosophy class and asked for me. Children whispered, "You're in trouble."

Of course, I wasn't afraid of Miss McKagg. She was a friend. I was scared, though, that she was going to tell me one of my family had died.

After she brought me to her office, she began, "Teacher Henderson told me you threw a wad of paper when you thought he wasn't looking. Other teachers have come to me with similar complaints. Can't you listen and behave a little better?"

"But it's so hard for me," I said in my best English. "Philosophy and literature . . ."

"What about that new poem by Longfellow? The one they are using in your literature class?"

"The Song of Hiawatha? I love that poem. It is about my Ojibwe people, though he got a few things wrong."

"How about Homer and Shakespeare?"

"Please, Miss McKagg, I have no idea what they're talking about. And, sorry to say, I don't care."

"Oh, Mary." Miss McKagg nodded, looking as sad as if her favorite aunt had just died.

Wanting to make her feel better, I said in my cheeriest voice, "I'll try, Miss McKagg, I'll listen."

The months rolled by, and I noticed I had been at McGraw for two years. I was fourteen.

Miss McKagg gave me chance after chance, but when, out of boredom, I took the braided hair of a girl in front of me and snipped off a chunk, I knew I had gone too far. The next day Miss McKagg called me to her office and informed me with tears in her eyes; "We have to let you go, Mary. Your behavior . . . it hurts me to see you struggle," she broke off.

I felt relieved, sad, and shocked all at once.

Then, Miss McKagg pulled out a big box from under her desk. "I have something for you, though. Remember the clothing you admired when Miss Bloomer came to talk about women's rights?"

I ripped open the package and hoped it would be—it was—a pair of bloomers! White with little pink bows.

I looked at Miss McKagg with love.

"Remember," she said, "Miss Bloomer said these pants are freeing women from tight corsets."

"How could I forget? I clapped so hard at the assembly I got into trouble. But it was worth it," I said with a wink.

Although my heart was heavy when I walked to my dormitory to tell my friends, Miss McKagg's gift had lightened my load. The girls cried and said they would miss me. We hugged and promised to write, though we never did.

McGraw sent me home when the term ended, so I could travel with another girl to Syracuse. The school sent a letter for my aunt and uncle to meet me there. A carriage took us to the train, and I bought a ticket from money Samuel sent me. He had heard from the headmistress. In his letter, he wrote how disappointed he was in my behavior, but ended the note saying, "I will find another school for you."

Leaving McGraw, I only had a few belongings wrapped in a blanket. However, I made sure to bring the bloomers. Would I ever wear them? Maybe not, but they would remind me of Miss McKagg and her kindness, even if McGraw couldn't keep me.

As our train pulled into Syracuse, I stared out the window and saw Uncle Ogima and Aunt Sarah on the platform. Wide-eyed, they looked like frightened children. The iron beast had that effect on people at first.

I was embarrassed by the way they were dressed. With their buckskin leggings, my auntie and uncle looked out of place, in this white man's city. They tried to fit in by wearing some new fashions. Uncle wore a tall black hat with a brim, but had added a red feather. Auntie wore a flowered cotton dress with a gray sweater, but her long braids and beaded necklace said "Indian." I must have looked just as mixed up. Though I wore my buckskin dress, I had on black boots because I had outgrown my moccasins. My hair was cut short.

This was the first time in two years I had seen my family. The other children from McGraw had gone home for breaks, or their parents had visited them. My family hadn't wanted to make the long trip. I'm not their real daughter, I reminded myself.

Aunt Sarah forced a smile. I hugged her but her arms stayed at her sides.

Uncle Ogima only grunted a few words.

We took a line boat filled with sweet-smelling apples. It was such a sparkling day; the canal reflected the green of the trees, the blue of the sky, and the purple of the lilacs. It reminded me of when Nimaamaa first opened her bags of seed beads, and I was amazed at how they sparkled. But, regardless of the clear skies above, a dark cloud of disappointment hung over our little group. I was evolving into a failure, and we all knew it.

When we got back to the Falls, I had another nightmare. I was running fast down train tracks just ahead of a roaring steam engine. I kicked out my leg, like I was running, and woke up Abequa. I told her I was having a bad dream and she put her arm around me, though less lovingly than before. My auntie woke up, but didn't bother to fetch a dream catcher. I guess she thought she thought I was too old for that, even though I still felt like a child.

It was hard to fall back asleep. I didn't fit in at McGraw,

nor now with my own family. What happened to my uncle's sweet promise to take care of me?

When I turned onto my stomach, I heard a woman's voice. "You have me, Mary. You will always have me."

I sat up and looked around. "Abequa, did you say some-thing?"

"No," my cousin answered. She turned her back to me and pulled the blanket with her.

Dazed, I felt the voice was trying to comfort me, but it was so odd. I couldn't tell where it was coming from. Staring at our birch bark ceiling, I thought; The sudden gusts of wind, the white hand, now the voice. Is there something wrong with me? Somehow, though, I felt comforted by the voice.

Cleopatra

Marc Antony was true to his word. He did send for me. It was years later, and I ignored his letters imploring me to come to Tarsus. I was 28 at the time. So much had transpired in the last 14 years that I could scarcely comprehend the events.

I had been Queen of Egypt for a decade now. Occupying the throne had taken every bit of my strength. I had survived terrible setbacks. The first of these was my beloved father's death, just two years after he had shown me his will. He died a ruined man, broken by debt and his loss of dignity. I dutifully "married" my younger brother, Ptolemy XII. Though he was only 11 years old, his deceitful mind was already churning with plans to seize the throne for himself.

My brother was not alone in wanting me gone. He had many allies in Alexandria who resented that a woman ruled them. I would face this prejudice throughout my reign.

When I had first ascended to the throne, Egypt's finances were in shambles. We owed the Romans 17 million drachmas!

The streets of Alexandria were in chaos, thanks to the unpaid soldiers the Romans had left behind. They were thugs, idle and lazy, taking what they wanted at the point of a sword. The outlying regions were no better when the Nile failed to flood. I faced food riots in the streets of Alexandria and used the army to keep the peasants from storming my palace. The leading citizens of Egypt scoffed at this teenage queen who had allowed the land to descend into anarchy.

Finally, they had had enough. When I was 21, my brother and his allies drove me from my throne. Surrounded by my few loyal subjects, I sailed up the Nile to Thebes, the historic heart of Egypt. I took Arsinoe with me to shield her from her brother's brutality. We briefly found refuge there, but soon heard Ptolemy's soldiers were marching south to meet us.

I had never dreamed of leaving Egypt but it had become too dangerous. Arsinoe and I made our way to Syria, where we found many sympathizers. I was forced to raise my own army to oppose Ptolemy. The daughter of Isis would now command troops. I also became one of the first female admirals of the ancient world.

We marched across the border into Pelousian, a city in the far east of Egypt. My force was no match for Ptolemy's, but I received salvation from an unlikely source—Julius Caesar was in the region. He was completing his conquest of our lands and had just defeated his last opponent in Rome's civil strife, loyalists to Pompei. Caesar next set his sights on restoring the Daughter of Isis to her rightful place.

Meanwhile, my deceitful sister had joined her brother to get rid of me. While they were massing for their attack on Pelousian, Caesar was passing through Judea. King Archelos gave Caesar the reinforcements he needed to launch an assault against the two young upstarts.

Ptolemy died in battle. He had insisted on fording the Nile at high water, wearing his heavy golden armor. The Romans found him buried in the mud. They captured Arsinoe and imprisoned her in the palace. The palace! That's where Caesar installed himself, in the finest chamber.

I admired that man. He was a skillful general and a wise ruler. Though he was more than three decades older, we shared a passion for knowledge and an appreciation of history. It was his idea to sail the royal barge up the Nile. Four hundred ships accompanied us. My flagship was 300 feet long, and so well appointed Caesar called it his "floating villa." I showed him the magnificent temples of Thebes. We sailed past massive statues at Memphis. Even these paled in comparison to the towering cliffs on the upper reaches of the river. Though he wouldn't admit it, Caesar was searching for the source of the Nile. When we neared the land of Ethiopia, I demanded we sail back to Alexandria.

Falling in love with a Roman seemed the remotest possibility, but his sharp mind and gentle kindness melted me. I even forgave him for destroying our library. I had been horrified when his soldiers carelessly caused the fire. The priceless writings of our greatest Greek philosophers perished in the flames.

I knew he had a wife back in Rome, a socialite, no less. When it came to choosing sides in Rome's civil war, many would turn against Caesar for the callous way he treated his wife, Calpurnia, and for his devotion to me. He had no children with his wife, but I bore Caesar's son on a June day. I was 22, Caesar was 53. We called our baby Caesarian. At the time, I thought he was the natural heir to his father's throne.

Caesar's behavior outraged the Romans and they had nothing but contempt for me. The Senate wearied of his long absence in Egypt and commanded him to return to Rome.

We were relaxing in my salon when the centurion came to find us. Caesar dandled his infant son on his knee and insisted the soldier admire Caesarian. The centurion looked perplexed. "Is this your grandson?" We both laughed as the baby gurgled. Caesar promised the bewildered emissary he would leave for Rome the next day.

After we were alone again with our son, I asked him, "Why must you leave so suddenly? Why can't you live out your life here? Won't you miss us?"

Caesar smiled. "Cleopatra, I would be quite content to remain here with you and watch my son grow. I find life here so agreeable."

"It shows in your face. Those lines you had, that coldness in your eyes, they are gone. I never saw a man so happy to be home."

"This can never be my home," he said, sadly. "I may look like a grandfather but my subjects will not let me enjoy my old age. They demand my attention now. There is strife in the streets of Rome and they're blaming me for lingering with you."

"If you cannot stay, please take us with you!" I implored. "I know the citizens of Rome despise me, but perhaps they will change their minds when they see me and our son by your side?"

"Don't worry, my love, I will see they show you proper respect," Caesar said, tenderly. "If only we were two commoners, how much happier we could be."

I laughed. "That's going too far. You would never be content to live in anything less than a palace."

Caesar gazed at our lavish surroundings, "Of course, you're right, but such heavy burdens come with all of this. I know you are in constant worry that someone will seize your power, perhaps that treacherous brother of yours. It is so much harder for you. My position is much more secure. In fact, some want to make me emperor."

I smiled. "I'm relieved. I feared that you also had enemies."

"Can't we speak of something else," Caesar said, warmly. "Let's enjoy our son, before it's time for his nap." He gently placed Caesarian on the rug and joined him on the floor. I found the sight quite comical. "I am glad to see you're still a boy. Perhaps I can get you a toy?"

Caesar gazed up at me, his eyes filled with tenderness. "Yes, you can give us toy swords. When Caesarian is old enough, I'll teach him to fight."

"Is that all men think of? I was going to show him how to ride."

"Oh, so he'll be in the cavalry riding alongside Marc Antony?" Caesar sighed. "What kind of parents are we? He can barely crawl and we already have him wearing armor. Speaking of that, I am leaving four legions behind to protect your throne." He stroked Caesarian's head. "Just wait until we get to Rome and they see what a splendid 'grandson' I have, and his enchanting mother."

"I'd be content not to be spat upon in the streets," I answered. "Do not flatter me like this in Rome. It will harden their hearts against you. Besides, my place is here. If need be, I will raise Caesarian alone."

We sailed to Rome, doting on our dear son. Like Isis, I was an unmarried mother, a goddess, with a single child. The Romans did not receive us well in the Eternal City. I did take pleasure, though, when Caesar paraded my wretched sister through its streets. He treated my youngest brother a bit better, imprisoning him in a Roman villa. As Caesar resumed his rule, I could see that I had influenced him. He immediately set about building a library.

This project didn't meet with any opposition, but when he proposed erecting a statue of me in the Temple of Venus, the populace was outraged. He went ahead anyway, casting my naked likeness in gold. Hatred for Caesar ignited among the people, and Cicero fanned the flames. It all came to a horrible end, when his cowardly "friends"

111

stabbed him on the senate floor. His devoted subordinate, Marc Antony, vowed revenge.

PART SIX
DISCOVERY

Mary Edmonia Lewis
Fifteen to Twenty Years Old
1859 - 1864

After I was forced to leave school, I went back to selling my once-praised souvenirs. But my heart was not in it. I no longer used the "orphan" bit with the tourists, because I was getting too old to play on their pity.

Going to my rock was the only thing that gave me comfort. Every day, after selling, I visited what I considered my only friend. Sitting cross-legged on the dirt, I told the rock how I felt. I mostly talked about how I didn't know what to do or where to go with my life.

One day Abequa came to sit next to me.

"You sure like this spot."

I laughed and said, "Yes, my rock and I are the best of friends."

"You're different since you came back, Mary."

"You've changed, too. Really, everyone in our band seems strange. Is it me? Am I making their life so miserable?"

"No, it's not you. We did miss you for a while, your lively spirit and the beautiful moccasins you made."

"Did you sell less after I left?" I asked, hopefully.

"Yes, but we're still making a little money," my cousin said. "The problem is that more white men are moving here. Samuel was right: they are making us buy our own land. At least, that is what my father hears when he goes to the trading post."

"And our family doesn't have the money to buy it?"

Abequa didn't answer. She picked up a stick and drew a simple face in the dirt.

"Is everyone afraid?" I asked.

"Nothing bad has happened yet, but everyone's worried."

"If we lose our land, we can always join our grandparents on the Credit River Reservation," I said, half-kiddingly.

Abequa frowned. "I will never live like that."

~❧~

My talk with Abequa picked up my spirits. It was even better than talking to my rock. She talked back, and her words were kind and helpful. Yet, I still was unsettled, and hoped to hear from Samuel soon.

One evening, my uncle brought me a letter from the trading post and dropped it on my lap. A letter from Samuel!

Dear Mary,

I found a new school for you to attend. I think you will like it and I pray that you will finish. Now that you can read, write, and do math, you will do well there, if you behave. Besides, you are 15 now, almost an adult. The school is called Oberlin College, in Oberlin, Ohio.

Please let me know if you are willing to go, and I will send a letter with directions to the school. I have already written them, and they said they would take you this September.

All my love,
Samuel

I let out a joyful cry, which startled my subdued relatives. When I told Abequa what the letter said, she hugged me.

Uncle Ogima shrugged, "Do we have to take you there?"

"Don't worry about getting me there. Samuel will send directions." All my travel adventures—by canoe, longboat, train, and stagecoach—told me I could do this.

"And will you behave this time?" Aunt Sarah asked.

I nodded.

Nokomis muttered, "We'll see."

After I wrote back to Samuel and got directions, I became scared about going alone. I would have to take a steamboat from Buffalo across Lake Erie to Cleveland. Oberlin sent daily stagecoaches there in September to pick up students.

My fear rolled away as the steamboat pulled away from the pier. With its big paddle going round and round, it glided ever so gracefully across the lake. When big waves came, the steamboat sliced right through them. And, to my pleasure, this boat carried barrels of grain and maple syrup—no murdered trees.

After the nine-hour trip, we reached Cleveland, where I waited for the stagecoach. When two other students and I climbed in, we were in high spirits. In no time, though, we winced with pain as the stage bumped violently over the lumpy trail. It took us two days to get to Oberlin, the place where I hoped to find success.

My spirits fell a little when I met the headmistress, Mrs. Dascomb. Sitting behind her big wooden desk, she wore a mean look along with a beige dress, a dull-colored shawl, a white lacey collar, and a frilly gray bonnet. Her features would have been pretty, if she didn't frown so much. She was nothing like my sweet Miss McKagg. Mrs. Dascomb held her nose so high, you would think that it was held up by a clothespin.

She shuffled through some papers and studied one in particular. "I see you're an orphan, Miss Lewis. We are required to place you on probation and you must live at a home where you will be closely supervised.

Thanks. I feel so welcome.

"You will live with 11 other girls in the home of Reverend John Keep and his wife. Mr. Keep is on Oberlin's board of trustees, and he cast the deciding vote to secure admission of girls as well as colored students to our school. You would do well to listen and show him the respect he deserves."

I felt a yawn coming but held it back. My new headmistress recited the classes I had to take: composition, rhetoric, botany, algebra, the Bible, and linear drawing.

Thank God for the drawing class. I could use my hands!

When I saw the Keeps' home, it reminded me of a bigger version of Captain Mills' white frame house. Chubby, white-haired, little Mrs. Keep greeted me warmly. "Come in, Mary. They told us you were coming. It is so nice to see you." Mrs. Keep showed me into the parlor and I met the other girls. When I set eyes on them, I was disappointed to see that I would have to wear a black dress with a frilly white collar, and a short, ugly hairstyle. What was it with white people and their dislike for bright colors?

But, once I got to know the girls and they got used to me, we had a good time together. We worked hard in our classes and listened to our teachers. But we could laugh and talk freely at the Keeps' house. The reverend was as kind as his wife.

I was the only non-white living there. Though I looked colored, I still saw myself as Ojibwe. I found myself making jokes about my heritage, and getting some laughs from the girls. Just like at McGraw, I would carry my pouch around and tell them that I had a magic Indian potion. I would sprinkle herbs on them. They thought it was funny.

My first month of classes went smoothly. I thought, I can handle this.

Then everything exploded, although it didn't have anything to do with me this time. It involved a man named John Brown. He was the son of the founder of the college.

We gathered in Clara's room and discussed the reasons for the excitement.

Christina said, "John Brown wanted to get the slaves to rise up and rebel."

Maria agreed, "But it didn't work out. The slaves didn't join him. Two of John Brown's sons and some colored men were killed. Now he's in jail. They may hang him."

"Where did all this happen?" I asked.

Maria knew the most. "A place called Harper's Ferry in West Virginia. It's where they keep guns for the soldiers."

"So, John Brown wanted the slaves to come there and get the guns?"

"Yes, but they didn't come," said Christina.

Mrs. Keep heard us talking and joined in. "I can't believe these well-meaning men were killed by United States soldiers. How could President Buchanan have allowed it? The Negro students, our faculty—we're all shocked. I don't know what's going to happen now."

No one had an answer. Slowly, we went back to our rooms to study.

It felt good to be in a place where people actually cared about coloreds.

A trial was held over Christmas break and the decision was made to hang John Brown from a tree. As usual, I was one of the handful of students who stayed at school. When John Brown was hung, all the bells on campus rang for a whole hour.

I had this vision of a tree forced to strangle the life out of an innocent man. My family would have been outraged. That tree had a soul. I had a nightmare about white people hanging me from a tree. The tree spoke up; "No, no, I will not let you do it!" The mob was so shocked that they ran off."

On Christmas Day, I joined the Keeps at a memorial service for the colored men from town. One was killed in battle and the other was hung with John Brown. It was supposed to be a happy season but Oberlin overflowed with grief.

Something in me stirred; a desire to bring to light the evil suffered by slaves and to shine a light on whites like John Brown who tried to free them. I didn't know yet what I would do, but I knew I would do something, someday.

❧

Two years passed, and in April of 1861 a battle broke out between the North and South at Fort Sumter in South Carolina. Our new president, Abraham Lincoln, had gotten 75,000 soldiers from the North to take on the South.

We continued to study and tried to block out the war, but many were worried about their fathers and brothers. Sometimes, they would call a girl out of class, and the rest of us would worry for her. Or a boy would be called out, and we would never see him again.

❧

As the war continued, we realized we needed to make the best of it. Like all the girls in our rooming house, I was becoming a young woman; I discovered some things about myself.

From what the girls said, I was a good artist. They liked to look at my latest work from my linear drawing class.

They also appreciated my sense of humor. Sometimes I pulled pranks, harmless ones. One day, Reverend Keep gave me his opinion about these shenanigans. The girls were on break, and all was quiet when he came to my door. In his usual soft tone, he asked, "Why don't you come to my office, and let's have a little chat?"

I froze for a moment. But when we got to his office and sat down, I saw that he still had a calm, cheerful expression.

After he asked how I was doing with my studies, Reverend Keep said, "I see you have the gift of making people laugh, and that is a good thing, Little One." He often used that nickname for me—it fit, since I was shorter than the other girls. "But I sense that sometimes your frivolity comes from a need for attention."

I felt the need to defend myself. "Is that so bad, sir? Life can be dull. We all need to laugh sometimes. I don't know about any need for 'attention.' "

He continued in his fatherly way, "I know you haven't had it easy, being an orphan, and your family unable to visit. Under such circumstances, anybody would need a little extra attention."

"When you put it that way, Reverend, it doesn't sound so bad."

"The only reason I bring it up, Mary, is that I don't want your need to be liked to lead you to do something you might regret."

"Thanks for your concern, sir. I'll think about it." When I left his office, I was so relieved. I thought he might have found the bottle of wine I had hidden in my room.

I couldn't go home for Christmas, but I wanted to have some kind of celebration.

If I had thought more about Reverend Keep's advice, I would have stayed out of trouble. I let my so-called "friends," Maria and Christina, push me into doing something I didn't think was wise, but was supposed to be fun.

The three of us had made a pact we would not tell anyone, ever, of our scheme for sending the girls out on their date. Let's just say it had something to do with the wine, my medicine pouch, and some foolishness the three of us planned to make their date more exciting.

After it all went wrong, I spent weeks lying in my bed, recovering from the beating those vicious boys gave me. I wrote to Samuel about the girls getting deathly ill and the charges against me. I told him about the attack, but made it sound less serious than it was. I concluded by saying, "I hope you don't think I let you down again."

Loving me as he did, Samuel took my side. He wrote, "I'm so sorry for all of the trouble you've been through. Let me know if there's anything I can do to help."

A Manitou, Lwa, or angel must have been watching over me, because an Oberlin graduate and the city's only colored lawyer, John Mercer Langston, volunteered to defend me. Reverend Keep told me that Mr. Langston had once been a slave. He had overcome many hardships to become a lawyer. Like me, he had a mother who was half-Indian and half-colored.

Mrs. Keep showed Mr. Langston into my room a few days before the trial. Although he looked young, his dress gave him the look of a much older man. He wore a fancy black brocade suit complete with vest, white shirt, and tie. Even white people respected him. He had been elected to the town council and board of education.

He took my hand as I lay in bed. "Miss Lewis, I am so sorry that you suffered such cruel treatment. I wish we knew who did this to you."

I tried to be a brave Ojibwe, but I let out a sob as I said, "I guess they thought they were paying me back."

"It was wrong for them to take the law into their own

hands," he said, sternly. Then, after a few moments, he asked, "Could you tell me what happened, what you were up to with your roommates?"

"I'm sorry, but I took an oath with the girls that I wouldn't tell."

Worry wrinkled his handsome features, but then he said, "I'll take your case, regardless."

Two days later, he returned to my bedside and said he had a solid defense for me and that I did not have to testify.

"Try to get your strength back. I'll need you in court, but you won't have to take the stand."

As I lay in bed, Clara told me that Oberlin's newspapers were buzzing about what had happened with the girls. "I guess some people have always been against Oberlin for opening its doors to coloreds and Indians. They say this incident shows it was a mistake. But others say race has nothing to do with it. Nevertheless, everyone is talking about you."

I said, in a mock-haughty way, "I never knew I would be so famous."

Clara groaned, like she did whenever I made a stupid joke.

Imagining the trial horrified me. All those white faces staring at me, probably thinking, See! Her color made her a killer!

The trial started a month later. My broken legs had not healed, and my ribs still hurt. Clara, with three of my classmates, carried me into the courtroom. People gasped when they saw me in my condition.

The courtroom was packed. Surprisingly, there were coloreds as well as whites. I would have died if I had had to sit in the witness chair; all those curious eyes.

They accused me of attempted murder. The fathers of the girls claimed I put "Spanish Fly," a so-called aphrodisiac, into some spiced wine and gave it to the girls before their sleigh ride. Mr. Langston argued that this could not be proven, because no tests of their stomach contents were conducted after the girls became ill. Nobody could argue with that. The judge dismissed the case for lack of evidence.

In the following weeks, Clara stood by me, but others avoided me. When I was strong enough, I went to a skating party. I was met with an iciness colder than any frozen pond.

To make matters worse, the owner of an art supply store accused me of stealing some prized brushes and a picture frame. I didn't steal his brushes, but I must admit I took the frame. I had temporarily lost touch with my brother and had no money. While I was looking around the store, I put the frame under my jacket. I needed it for a drawing I made for Clara. I thought, Other students have money; they can buy nice things. Why not me?

A bright spot came when I visited my old drawing teacher, Miss Georgianna Wyett.

"I'm so glad you dropped by, Mary. I hope you have kept up with your drawing."

I thought, At least she still cares about me.

"I've only done a little drawing. I'm so busy with my other classes."

She looked up from the papers she was grading. "You have a gift, Mary."

I glowed. "I've been told that before."

Several sculptures on her shelves grabbed my attention. They were the heads of important-looking white men.

"I love those!" I said.

She told me how a well-known sculptor, Hiram Powers, had exhibited a statue of a statue of a Greek slave in Cincinnati ten years ago. It was done in the old Classical style and caused a sensation. "Now artists have been sculpting these busts of heroic Greeks and Romans. People have been buying them like crazy."

"Ah," I said. "That looks like something I'd like to do."

"Who knows?" Miss Wyett said. "Someone who can draw like you—anything is possible."

❧

The death knell for my education sounded on the day Mrs. Dascomb called me into her office. I swear that if anyone ever calls me into their office again, I will run for the nearest way out.

In an icy voice, she began, "Mary, there has been so much suspicion cast upon you with the court case and now the thievery, I cannot have you remaining at our college. You are ruining our good name."

She leaned forward and looked me firmly in the eyes. "If you register for classes next semester, your application will be turned away. You can finish this term, but that will be it."

"But, Mrs. Dascomb, I only have two semesters left. Why are you doing this?"

"The board asked me to set the standards for our Ladies' Department. They will back me."

"How do you know?"

"Do you want to go through another hearing, young lady?"

I stalked out, fighting the urge to slam her door.

I ran to the Keeps' house. I don't belong at Oberlin, at McGraw, or with my family. Where will I go? What will I do?

Tears streamed down my face. I smothered them with my mittens. When I got to the Keeps' house, I collapsed on my bed. Mrs. Keep ran into my room to see what was wrong. When I told her, I couldn't believe what came out of her mouth. "That Mrs. Dascomb! May she rot in hell!"

A bit shocked by her outburst, she sat down to calm herself. "I will speak with Mr. Keep."

I had never felt such despair. I longed for the loving touch of my mother and father. I didn't have anyone to care about me.

At least that is what I thought, but Reverend Keep came through and saved me. The school still would not allow me to graduate, but he guided me in a new direction.

He sent a letter of introduction to William Lloyd Garrison in Boston. He was the president of the American Anti-Slavery Society and a prominent journalist. After

Garrison wrote back and asked what I might like as a job, Mr. Keep replied that I would like to work as an artist. He asked Garrison to put me in touch with a Boston artist who might need an assistant. When Mr. Garrison wrote back to Reverend Keep, he sent the address of a Mr. Brackett, who was a sculptor. He would be willing to give me a try.

Boston was far away, but being an expert in all forms of transportation, I wasn't frightened . . . much.

I accepted Samuel's offer of help and asked him to send me money for train tickets and lodging. Samuel wrote that he was making a fortune from the Gold Rush in California and could easily pay for my trip. I didn't contact my family at Niagara Falls. If I told them about Oberlin, I could just imagine their disgust.

Mrs. Dascomb said I should finish the semester and then go to Boston with a student who had made the trip several times. Everything in my heart made me want to leave Oberlin immediately, but I forced myself to finish my classes. It was so painful to sit there, knowing I couldn't graduate. I was leaving botany class one day, when my colored friend, Matilda, stopped me. She had helped carry me into court.

"Is there anything wrong, Mary?"

"I'm fine, just fine," I answered sharply. "I'm leaving soon."

"Before you go, you should come see me. I'm at the Van Doren house."

I never took her up on her offer. I felt walls encircling me, blocking out everyone, the good people along with the bad.

Before I left Oberlin, Clara came to my room. I motioned for her to sit on my bed.

In a whisper, I told her, "I have a secret. I need to talk to someone. You're the only one I trust here. It will be our secret. You don't mind?"

Clara leaned toward me, wide-eyed. "Is it about the girls?"

"No, I can't even tell you about that."

Clara's face fell, but I continued, "You're going to think I'm crazy." I kept my voice low. "Remember, right after I was beaten?"

"How could I forget?"

"Something appeared that night. A white—it was like fog—came in through a crack in my window. It turned into a woman sitting—I don't know—on a chair or throne."

"You were probably just confused, Mary. I mean, you went through a lot."

"I can see why you would think that, but a few years ago a white hand also appeared."

"It couldn't be a ghost," Clara countered. "There's no such thing. That's what my parents always tell me." But the slight shake to her voice said she wasn't sure.

"And once I heard a voice, but no one was there," I said.

"What did it say?"

"'You have me, Mary. You will always have me.'"

"Strange."

"And one more thing. I have heard a sound, a few times, that no one else has heard."

"What kind of sound?"

"A strong rush of wind that lasts, oh, just a few seconds."

"When did these strange things happen?"

I had never considered this. Finally, I said, "It's always an important time, like when my father and mother died. Or when I go on a scary long journey. Or when I feel alone."

"Hmm, Reverend Keep would say it was the Good Lord telling you not to give up."

"As much as I love the Lord, I don't think it's Him." I thought for a moment. "But I believe that whoever or whatever it is wants me to keep me going."

Clara shivered. "This is giving me goosebumps."

Then she said, "You're my friend, and wherever you go or whatever you do, I will always care about you." Clara giggled. "Even if at times you are a little odd."

I laughed with my friend. Then, half-kidding and half-serious, I said, "Please don't tell anyone about this, or they will send me away."

"I won't. Besides, who would believe me?"

"One more thing. I know you're getting married right after graduation. I want to give you your wedding gift before I leave."

I pulled out my stolen picture frame with the drawing I had made of a small statue I admired in Ms. Wyett's office. It was of Uranus, the goddess of music. Since Oberlin was proud of its music school and Clara sang in the choir, it would bring back good memories. My art teacher said I did it in "the Classical style," because the goddess was dressed in lots of drapery and looked god-like.

After studying the drawing, Clara pressed it to her chest and said, "When I look at this, it will always remind me of you."

A week before I left, Mrs. Keep gave me a carpetbag to carry my valuables—a few remnants of my Ojibwe jewelry and my never-worn bloomers. I went to the general store and used money from Samuel to buy a skirt, a white blouse, a jacket, and a scarf. I would be a stylish woman! Hopefully, the clothes would help me fit in when I got to Boston.

The stagecoach pulled up to the Keeps' to take us to the train station. While the horses neighed, I shared a last moment with Mrs. Keep and Clara.

"I will only remember the good and try not to think about the bad at Oberlin. I will never forget how kind you've both been and, of course, Reverend Keep." My voice suddenly became angry, "But I'll show Mrs. Dascomb." In a forceful voice, I said, "I will be somebody!"

Remembering stories about my ancestors' war parties, I thought; As a true Ojibwe, I'll get revenge on her!

Rising from my chair and firmly grasping my carpetbag, I declared, "I'm starting over. I will never talk of how I was disgraced here. Mary Edmonia is gone. From now on I'm Edmonia—Edmonia Lewis!"

∾❦∾

There was no direct train to Boston; we had to transfer four times. A spell of hot weather had come to our region, so we had to leave the train windows wide open. Sparks from the train's coal-powered engine blew into our compartment and landed on our clothes. I ended up with about 15 burn holes in my new jacket. The student I traveled with was quiet and didn't look up from her book. This made me wonder: was she one of the many who thought I was a murderer?

During the ride, I saw Union soldiers marching down the road that followed the tracks. Would they come back alive?

There was one highlight. I perked up when a young Negro man with a bright smile and arms as strong as Samuel's entered our car. I was surprised that I could still feel attracted to a fellow, but I knew right then and there the fellow would have to be colored. In my nightmares, the eyes of my white attackers dripped with blood. Their teeth became fangs, and their hands turned into sharp blades.

I searched for an excuse to talk with the good-looking young man, but he got off before I could think of anything to say.

When we finally arrived, I made my way to a desk that said "Information." I gave the man at the desk the address of Mr. Brackett's studio. As if it pained him to share his precious information, the man muttered it was only eight blocks away, and told me how to get there.

I had never been in such a big, busy city. Horses and buggies hurried in every direction. The smoke and dirt choked me. I longed for the sweet smell of our tall pines back at Niagara. But I followed the directions and found myself staring at a larger-than-life statue. Thanks to my Oberlin education, I recognized it was Ben Franklin. I had never seen such a large sculpture. Someday I will make something like this!

Then I lost my way and asked busy people with impatient eyes for directions. Eventually, I found my way to the studio on Tremont Street. The door was open, and I saw a man working.

"Hello," I began. "I'm Edmonia Lewis. I believe Mr. Garrison sent you a letter of introduction about me."

Like any artist, Mr. Brackett didn't appreciate being disturbed in the act of creating.

"I hate to bother you, but Mr. Garrison said you might teach me. Hopefully, I can help at your shop."

Mr. Brackett looked me over. My hair was frizzy. I was sweating. The burn marks on my jacket embarrassed me. And my face felt full of soot. However, Mr. Brackett was no prize himself. His gray hair was as messy as mine. He wore the striped shirt and wool vest of our times, but was covered with white powder. He smelled like he hadn't had a bath for a month.

Mr. Brackett said, "All right, I'll see what you can do. Anything for Garrison. Sit down and I'll tell you about my work.

"I make busts of famous people. If you look over there, that's a bust of John Brown."

I walked over to the table for a closer look. He looked like a prophet from the Bible. Mr. Brackett had captured the fire in his eyes. "I know about him," I said over my shoulder.

"He was a great man. I visited him while he was in prison. I made measurements of his head."

"It's amazing!" You made him look like the true hero he was."

134

I had enough money from Samuel to take a room at a boarding house. When I returned to Mr. Brackett's studio the next morning, he gave me an assignment. "Here is a cast of a child's foot. If you can copy it in clay, I'll know whether you can be a sculptor."

Working with clay was new to me. I began with a big ball of it, and threw it down, hard, on the board. As I started to shape it, I squeezed the clay with both hands as if I was choking it.

Mr. Brackett stopped me. "Not so rough!"

"Don't worry," I reassured him. "This will be a masterpiece."

Brackett looked at me doubtfully.

I realized my hands were acting out my rage. But I couldn't tell Mr. Brackett or anyone else about Oberlin.

The words of my uncle came back; "Everything has a soul." I worked more gently with the poor clay.

One day, when Brackett left the studio on an errand, a visitor appeared in the doorway. Wearing a high-necked navy blue dress, white bonnet, and lacy collar, a woman with graying brown hair looked at me and said, "You must be Edmonia."

"Yes, but how did you know?"

"At one of our abolitionist meetings, Mr. Brackett mentioned you, his new promising artist."

I didn't know that I was "promising" or "his artist."

I asked her, in my most high-style manner, "And to whom do I have the pleasure of speaking?"

"My name is Lydia Child. I write newspaper articles and books."

"About what, may I ask?"

"The Civil War. The losses we report are so terrible, I'm trying to convince our readers it's worth it. I'm also trying to convince them that Negroes are just as valuable, and intelligent, as whites"

I was impressed.

"I'm working for the rights of Indians to keep their lands. I also believe women—we should have the same rights and opportunities as men."

I laughed. "Well, you've just summed me up. I'm colored, a woman, and an Indian."

"Ah," Lydia Child murmured. "But look at how far you've traveled and what you have accomplished."

"How do you know?" I asked, still surrounded by walls of suspicion.

"Why, Mr. Brackett told me all about you."

Mrs. Child prattled on; "I would like to interview you and feature your story in my Anti-Slavery newspaper."

"That's the one Mr. Garrison publishes?"

"Yes. I could talk about your work. I'll include the address of Mr. Brackett's studio so people can come and view and," she added with emphasis, "buy your art."

The saleswoman in me awakened. Just like at the Falls, I looked for any angle to sell my art. Smiling now, I said, "An interview would be fine."

With promises to return, Mrs. Child breezed out of the shop. If someone thinks I am adorable, I might as well take advantage of it.

〰️⚎〰️

Mr. Brackett had the obnoxious habit of constantly clearing his throat, and his breath smelled of garlic. But what a teacher! He gave me a damaged piece of marble, showed me how to use his sculpting tools, and let me at it.

While practicing on the marble, I finished my clay mold of the child's foot. Holding the foot in his hand, the usually bland Mr. Brackett said, "This is perfect! I think you might have what it takes."

Things were going well in my "job" at the studio. Then, one morning when I came to work, Brackett looked up from his latest creation and said, "I'd like a word with you, Edmonia."

I felt a cold panic. If he wants to speak to me in his office, I will run out the door.

He didn't. He just stared at me and said, "You've been stealing from me."

My mouth dropped open.

"Two weeks ago, I couldn't find one of my tools. I thought I had simply misplaced it. I blamed it on my disorganized ways. Last week, I discovered another tool missing. No one else has been here but you and me."

He kept staring.

I sat down. "All right, I did take them. I'm sorry."

"Why?"

"I've lost touch with my brother, Samuel. He sends me money when I need it. I don't know where he is now. So, I can't ask him for help."

"What does that have to do with my tools?"

"Honestly, I want to open my own workshop someday, when Samuel can help me. I knew I would need tools . . ." My voice trailed off.

Brackett said, "You don't seem to have any friends or family, other than this brother of yours. Is that right?"

"Yes."

"You're very independent and, I think, proud."

"True."

"If you need something, just ask. You have great talent. If you had asked for a tool or two, I would have given them to you. But you can't just take them."

As proud as I was, I felt ashamed. I couldn't hold back the tears.

Between sobs, I promised Mr. Brackett, "I will never, ever steal again." At that moment, I knew it was true. I gave up my life of thievery, but I always understood people who took things.

After our brief talk, Mr. Brackett let me get back to my work. I was feeling so alone. Then I heard that voice: "You have me, Mary. You will always have me."

I looked around the room and blurted out, "What?"

Mr. Brackett looked at me, puzzled. "Is there something wrong, Edmonia?"

I couldn't answer him. That night, it was hard to sleep. The voice was the same one I had heard before. I loved the feeling of being cared for, but by an invisible being?

One of Brackett's clients paid me eight dollars for the foot. Such a sum for my first sale!

Samuel finally got in touch, with his new address.

138

He sent enough money for me to open my shop. He was happy that I now had a "job."

I rented a studio in the building where Mr. Brackett worked. I hung out a tin sign; "EDMONIA LEWIS, ARTIST."

I had finally discovered my calling!

Cleopatra

WITH CAESAR'S DEATH, I NAIVELY thought our son would ascend to the throne. However, the senate named Caesar's nephew, Octavian, as Caesar's heir. I was fuming. Before I returned to Egypt, I removed another of my rivals: I poisoned my youngest brother. As usual, he was too impatient to wait for the taster. Now, only Arsinoe opposed me.

I was back in Alexandria when Marc Antony's letters found me. He was 42 years old now, and married to a noble woman named Fulvia. She knew her husband had mistresses but, like many wives of her day, she didn't protest. Though always fond of drink, Antony had become fat and sloppy, known for scandalous behavior when he was in his cups.

I ignored his letters, but when his most trusted aide visited my palace, he convinced me to go see Antony. I sailed the next day to Tarsus. My golden barge had purple sails. My legions of oarsmen drove the ship with silver oars. I reclined under a colorful canopy, careful not to betray that I suffered from seasickness. My fairest maidens trimmed the sails and steered the ship. My crew planted palm trees on deck to remind me of my eternal Egypt.

After we reached shore, I hosted an elaborate banquet

for Antony and his men. Musicians played, and dancing girls kept Antony's golden goblet from running dry. I hadn't seen him in years and was saddened by what he had become.

The next morning we strolled the shore, with servants holding fans to shield us from the sun. A contingent of Antony's soldiers followed at a discreet distance. Neither of us was feeling well. My face was still a bit greenish from the sea voyage. Antony's eyes were bloodshot, and he reeked of wine.

"Oh, Princess," he moaned, holding a hand to his brow.

"You can no longer address me that way," I snapped.

He winced. "Yes, My Queen, so much has happened since we last met."

"Yes," I said, imperiously. "You have become fat and friendless, exiled in a strange land."

He laughed derisively, "Cleopatra, you have become soft yourself. No one would mistake you for a boy."

I was annoyed. "My softness is the result of bearing Caesar's child. I didn't get this way from drunkenness." I lowered my voice. "It is not healthy to live like you do. You are destroying your good humors, your insides. You'll be dead at a young age."

Again, he scoffed. "Oh, I forgot, you wrote that well-regarded medical book. Let's see, what was the lofty title—you called it 'Cosmetics?'"

I recoiled at his sarcasm. "If you knew anything, you would know that what we eat and drink, our habits good and bad, show in our appearance. I have identified many diseases that I detect by examining a person's countenance.

The burst blood vessels in your nose tell me everything about how you live."

Antony smiled affectionately and took my hands. "I did not invite you here to quarrel, or for you to lecture me. You must know how desperate my situation is."

"Yes, I have heard," I said with concern. "Your soldiers have deserted you because you can no longer pay them. You have no army or fleet and your enemies surround you on all sides. Am I supposed to save you?"

"Cleopatra, it is not just my skin I'm trying to save. You are also in danger from Octavian's forces. Sad as it appears, we only have each other."

He stopped on an outcropping and shielded his eyes as he gazed at the sea. "He is assembling a fleet right now, and someday there will be enemy sails on the horizon."

I really did feel sorry for this pitiful man, the greatest orator who had ever spoken on the senate floor. "Is it ships that you need?" I offered. "I have 140 transports and 60 warships, all fully supplied."

Antony grinned. "Perhaps I should call you Admiral?" I didn't smile. He got serious again. "We will need much more than that to hold off Octavian."

I saw now how far Antony had fallen. "You mean my navy is insufficient to save your skin, as you put it. Should I also empty my treasury to pay for your army?"

Antony said nothing, but stared at me with the saddest eyes. My heart softened a bit. I couldn't forget that he had restored my father to the throne and protected me at the palace. I also saw that neither of us could stand alone against Octavian.

"Consider it done," I said, coldly. "I can't stand to see you like this."

"Cleopatra," he protested. "You know that you mean more to me than all the ships and treasure you possess. Don't you remember that I confessed my love for you at our last meeting?"

"Yes," I said, wistfully. "It didn't make sense then but it makes sense now. You need something."

Antony suddenly dropped to his knees and embraced me around the waist. Horrified, I dismissed the servants and waved away the guard.

"My Queen," he sobbed, thick tears soaking his beard, "It's not your riches I want—it's your spirit I crave." His shoulders shook. I had heard that Antony was unafraid to cry but I was unsettled by the sight.

"Please," I said raising him to his feet. "If what you say is true, you may someday possess all of me. But, for now, this is a business arrangement. If we are going to be partners, you must refrain from this wine that is slowly poisoning you."

Antony laughed. "It's easy to swear off drink, when you feel the way I do this morning. He paused. "I will try, My Queen."

"I don't expect you to stop chasing servant women, but please be subtle."

"Cleopatra," he said, quietly embracing me and nuzzling my neck. "You are the only woman that has stolen my heart." He didn't mention how he felt toward his wife but I had that feeling again of falling in love with an older married man—another Roman, no less.

Over the next few years, Antony and I proved to be a good team. He was a brilliant military strategist and I had the riches to pay for his plans. We assembled 800 ships and 100,000 men. We had allies in several kingdoms, including Judea, where Archelos and his son, Herod the Great, promised reinforcements and supplies.

We knew Octavian was also building up his forces. But he only had 200 ships and 80,000 soldiers. We thought having such a superior force would give us victory. In 31 BC, our fleet sailed to Actium to face Octavian's navy. My flagship was the most famous in antiquity. I called it Antonias, after my lover. Like my royal barge, it was rigged with purple sails. I commanded 60 ships.

Just before the Battle of Actium began, on September 2, I was on deck directing the crew when my eye was drawn to a swallow flitting above the deck. I followed its flight to where swallows had fashioned a nest in the upper deck. Such an omen! The sacred bird of Isis had taken shelter on my ship. I thought nothing could keep Antony and myself from victory.

When we began our assault, Antony's ship became disabled. He came aboard the Antonias and remained at my side the rest of the battle. Though we had overwhelming numbers, we had hastily assembled our fleet. We could not supply it with seasoned officers. Instead, we enslaved merchant sailors to serve. They were no match for Octavian's well-trained crews.

As I watched the Roman fireballs find their mark, my thoughts were of Egypt. I was more concerned about defending my kingdom than in defeating Octavian.

The Romans branded me, the Queen of Egypt, and Antony, as cowards! For fleeing the battle. After I died, they used this example to distort my image. I became a caricature of a seductress luring Romans to their ruin.

We sailed south for three days, heading to my homeland. The fleet we had hurriedly left behind lacked leadership and offered little resistance to Octavian. Many of the crews defected to his navy.

As the world collapsed around us, we received more bad news. Herod had deserted us and was allying himself with Octavian. I wasn't surprised that he, our last "friend" in the Middle East but ever the traitor, deceived us.

As our ship plied the waters, Antony was useless. He brooded alone on the foredeck for three days, refusing to talk to me or anyone else. I had seen Antony's dark moods before. They made him insufferable. This same man, though, when he was in high spirits, could make me laugh like no other. We both liked the same kind of fun: dressing up in rags and startling strangers in Alexandria.

This was the Antony I loved, and I bore him three delightful children. I knew I must save them along with my throne. I wondered if my children by Antony could tell that I loved my son by Caesar more than them. It was certainly true. The Romans may have denied Caesarean his rightful place but I was preparing him to take the throne of Egypt.

When Antony and I sailed into the harbor of Alexandria, the terrible news from the Battle of Actium had not yet reached the capital. I flew the flags of victory and Antony and I pretended to the people that we had triumphed over the hated Romans. They weren't taken in for long.

Egypt was in poverty. It had never recovered from the heavy debt my father had imposed on his people. Now, I had emptied the treasury to finance our forces. Desperate, I confiscated the riches of the wealthy. If they resisted, I had them executed. I even robbed the gold and silver treasures from our temples. I hoped that Isis would understand.

I was once the richest woman in the world and now I was bankrupt. There was famine in Egypt and I could do nothing for my starving subjects.

Despite all the setbacks, I remained strong and resolute to keep my kingdom intact. I wish I could have said the same for Antony. When we arrived in Alexandria, he refused to set foot in the palace. He built a rough shelter on the beach and isolated himself inside. When he spoke at all, it was of suicide. In fact, he was attempting to take his life when his aides stopped him. For his own safety, they led him to the palace.

I couldn't worry about Antony: I had my own radical course to take. I decided to abdicate the throne for Caesarian. I would then flee Egypt and leave him to rule. My plan was to transport my ships across the desert to the Red Sea. I would then sail to a new life in India. I never found out if it was possible to carry ships across the sands, because a traitor first set fire to my fleet. Octavian had trapped me in Alexandria and I had to face him alone.

Antony tried one last effort to defeat the Romans. He dispatched the remnants of his fleet to fight them. His entire navy defected. Powerless against his foe, Antony took out his anger on Arsinoe. I had approved of the execution of my final rival. But did Antony have to employ such a cruel method—having my younger sister dragged to her death?

I thought I could deal with Octavian alone. I sent him my last sums of money, with a message asking him to install Caesarian on the throne. The scoundrel kept the money but sent no reply. Instead, he sent a message to me suggesting I eliminate Antony. Seeing no way out, I commanded my slaves to begin building my tomb on the palace grounds.

While they were working, I used my medical knowledge to collect a variety of poisons. I was looking for one that was quick-acting, painless, and untraceable. Meanwhile, Octavian's army marched across Judea. Herod showered them with wine, water, and money. Antony dispatched his cavalry to meet Octavian at Egypt's border. Once again, his soldiers betrayed him, as his men joined the invaders.

The Romans easily captured the city of Pelousian, in eastern Egypt. From there, Octavian sent emissaries to me, to negotiate the surrender of my kingdom. These talks dragged on for five months. I could no longer tolerate seeing Antony in misery. So, I moved from the palace into my tomb. I brought all my jewels and treasures with me. My statue of Alixir was my beacon, glittering in the slanting sunlight.

I told my servants to lie to Antony that I had succumbed to poison. He took the news the way I expected. Antony had his most trusted friend run him through with a sword. He did not die. So, I commanded that he be brought to me.

I watched through the high window of my sepulcher as my servants carried Antony from the palace.

When they reached my crypt, three of my maidens hoisted him with ropes to my window. A large crowd gathered to watch the bloody spectacle. My lover could barely speak. "My Queen," he gasped as rivulets of blood spilled from his mouth, "I am dying an honorable man." He coughed and spat blood. "Killed . . . by a Roman." He barely got these words out before his eyes rolled back. I stroked his forehead; Marc Antony was dead at 53, and I would soon join him.

With their father gone, Antony's children were helpless. Octavian seized them as hostages. He tried to force me to accept his terms. Though he never said it, my surrender meant I would live out my days as a slave. I was determined to die as a queen.

My servants bathed me and dressed me in my imperial costume, including my purple robe, glittering bracelets, and royal headdress. They prepared a sumptuous feast. It included some especially delicious figs. I then locked myself in my tomb. Octavian and his men found me there. It was August 10, in 30 BC. I was 39 years old. Octavian discovered tiny puncture wounds in my right arm. He noticed a suspicious basket nearby, but no one would ever know how the Queen of the Nile ended her reign.

PART SEVEN
REALIZATION

Edmonia Lewis
Twenty to Twenty-Eight years Old
1864 - 1872

EVERY MORNING, AS I WALKED from my boarding house to my shop, I heard newsboys calling out how many Union soldiers were killed or captured. At my age, I would rather have laughter surrounding me and a look or two from a nice-looking fellow, but I knew that wasn't likely with all the trouble around us.

One frigid Boston afternoon, Mrs. Child pushed opened the door and blew into my studio, fittingly with a gust of wind and snow.

"You must be freezing, Mrs. Child. Sit by the fire. Oh, and thank you for that nice article about me in The Broken Fetter."

"You are quite welcome." Mrs. Child shivered. She hurried to the fire, took off her gloves, and rubbed her hands over the flames. She talked of the war.

"Have you heard, Edmonia, about the young white colonel, Robert Gould Shaw?"

"No. What's so special about him?"

"He's leading the first ever regiment of colored soldiers."

I knew the conversation would have to do with something about race. "That's very impressive."

"People thought that the coloreds might not make such good soldiers, but, of course, I knew they would be up to the job, just like any white men."

"Of course, you did," I said, and hoped that she would not note my sarcasm.

A few months later I was working on a bust of Abraham Lincoln. It was a sunny spring day. I left my door open to breathe in the sweet smell of cherry blossoms. My concentration was broken by the clumping of what sounded like a horse's hooves, followed by a rhythmic clunking, the likes of which I had never heard before. I went to the doorway and saw a white man on a brown horse followed by a large group of marching colored men—Colonel Shaw and his regiment.

As Shaw approached, I strained to observe every detail about him. He hardly appeared old enough to lead a regiment. Sitting tall and stiff in his saddle, he looked quite handsome. His men, their backs straight as boards, marched behind him.

I rushed to my desk and sketched everything I remembered of Colonel Shaw. To me, and to many other coloreds, as well as whites, he was a hero.

Months later, newsboys shouted a story that commanded my attention. The Confederates had killed Colonel Shaw and half of his men when they made their courageous assault on Fort Wagner in Georgia.

Mrs. Child and her abolitionist friends couldn't give him enough glory. I decided to sculpt him.

That was all the rage in those days: choose a hero, imagine him looking noble, and carve him into stone. Ah, stone! I thought about my rock back at Niagara. How I would love to talk to it again!

But, for now, marble had to be my stone.

I sent a letter to Samuel asking him to send me money to buy a piece of marble about 36 inches long and 20 inches wide, to make a bust of the colonel.

All I had to guide me were my sketches and a bleary photo of Shaw in a newspaper. However, Mrs. Child knew the Colonel's parents well. I begged her to ask them for a picture of him I could copy.

"Edmonia, you know I have celebrated your talents in my newspaper stories and held you up as an example of what a colored person can accomplish. But I think you need more training before you set upon such an effort."

"I know I can capture his look, if only you would help me. I'll never forget his face; such dignity and courage."

"It's one thing to remember a look and another to chisel it into marble," she said in her usual superior tone. You will waste your dear brother's money if you ruin the marble."

"But, but, I have to try," I protested.

Mrs. Child ignored me. "I'm sorry. I'm leaving. I have to visit my sister. She's not feeling well."

Under my breath, I cursed her, with words even the devil might find shocking.

But when I was determined to do something, I did it.

I worked from my sketches to make the bust, first using a pitching tool to chip away at the marble. I hit the pitching tool with my mallet. Angry with Mrs. Child and carrying my other resentments, I pounded too fiercely. Then I remembered what Mr. Brackett had said about the way I manhandled the clay. I stepped away, took a few deep breaths, and collected myself. As I did so, I felt better and once again found joy in my work. I slowly cut away the marble and shaped Shaw's bust to look like the man I'd only seen for a few moments. I thought I had gotten him right.

My opinion was not wrong. His family loved it. I sold the marble bust for a large sum, as well as 100 plaster copies of it for 15 dollars each at the Colored Soldiers Fair in Boston.

With my eye on the market, I made terracotta medallions of leading abolitionists—John Brown, Charles Sumner, Wendell Phillips, and Colonel Shaw—that would sell in the North. I put an ad in the paper telling the public they could buy these keepsakes. It worked, and I had a steady parade of customers coming to my studio.

I saved most of my profits but also invested in some clothing that I was lusting after. Yes, lusting after. I bought a blue skirt, a white blouse with pretty layers of frilly lace, a white scalloped collar, and a broach with a rose on it. Instead of purchasing petticoats, like other women, I bought myself a pair of pink bloomers. I had kept a small scrap of the bloomers Miss McKagg had given me, in memory of her kindness, but I was determined to have a new pair for myself. Of course, I bought the traditional bonnet, but it was a small one and I kept it towards the back of my head, allowing my curly black hair to flow freely.

Sculptor Edmonia Lewis Displays Work in Boston
November 11, 1864

While in Boston, I met a woman who changed my life: Harriet Hosmer. A mannish-looking woman in her thirties, Harriet came to my studio one day with Mrs. Child.

Mrs. Child introduced her as "the greatest female artist of our century, perhaps of any century." She was in Boston to visit family and exhibit her work.

Harriet sculpted her pieces in Rome. Rome: home to great sculptors for centuries!

She looked me in the eye and said, "I would like to see your work."

I showed her around my studio. When she saw the

marble bust I was completing of a Civil War officer, she was taken aback.

"My goodness, you have it!"

"What? What do I have?"

"You have the ability to be a sculptor; a sculptor in the Classical tradition! You have captured this soldier's courage in his furrowed brow and the determined set of his mouth." She walked around the bust. "And you are polishing the marble to such a luster."

I knew what she said was true and that she was not just flattering me.

"Why don't you come to Rome, Miss Lewis, and join our group of female sculptors?"

Mrs. Child looked troubled. "Oh, but she has so much to learn. Edmonia has had very little formal training."

Harriet answered in an upbeat way. "We can teach her more, if she wants our help. But, you know what? I think she's ready to go!"

❧

Immediately, I dreamed of going to Rome. I sent a letter to Samuel, and then I talked with Mr. Brackett.

"Rome," he said wistfully. "What better place to study classical art and avail yourself of their fine Carrara marble. My one suggestion is to start in Florence. They have gorgeous churches. Michelangelo's David and Moses are there too. And Florence has our most outstanding American male sculptor."

"Who?"

"None other than—have you heard of Hiram Powers? I could send him a letter of introduction, if you'd like."

Hiram Powers—my art teacher had told me about him!

That night, I lay in bed, wide-eyed. I had enough money for a one-way voyage to cross the Atlantic. Florence would be the place to start. Then I could go to Rome to work with the greatest!

"So, Manitou, Lwa, ghost, or whoever you are, what do you think of this? You've talked to me, sent me gusts of wind, and even appeared to me! Perhaps it has been about the art. Do you think I should go to Rome?"

Nothing.

"Come on, now. What do you think?"

No answer.

~⊙~

Two months later, I traveled to Florence on my newest mode of transportation: an iron-hulled ship. The ocean was sometimes smooth but often rough. Gigantic waves crashed into our ship, but I did not panic. I'd made it through all my other journeys. I knew the captain would not risk lives if he thought things were unsafe. I trusted him more than some other people I knew.

After finally arriving on the coast of Italy, I took a carriage to Florence. When the driver reached the outskirts, he took a cobblestone street to the heart of the city. Gorgeous marble sculptures of prophets and apostles appeared in niches of buildings as frequently as signboards in Boston.

At the center of Florence, my eyes took in a large piazza featuring a tall, wide, marble church. I would have never guessed that a church could be built entirely of marble, thousands of rectangles of marble! Aside from the majesty of the Niagara forest, I had never seen such beauty.

Across the piazza was a smaller church, shaped as an octagon. It, too, was made of marble. The church had tall wooden doors covered with golden carvings of stories from the Bible.

"It's too much," I exclaimed.

The driver then took me down a side street to the residence of Hiram Powers.

When I arrived, Powers gushed, "You must be our American girl!"

After serving me wine and pastries, he showed me to a little room where I could stay until I found my own place. I hadn't had wine in a long time. As he guided me to my room, I did my best to hide my wobbliness.

The highlight of my stay at Powers' home was the tour of his studio. It contained one sculpture after another much like the ones I had seen in the streets. But there was something just a little more modern and polished about his work. I was entranced and perhaps a little shocked when I saw his sculpture of a woman with one sleeve of her dress coming down to expose her bare breast. We didn't see such artwork back home.

Powers noticed and said, "Edmonia, don't be embarrassed. Almost all classical Greek and Roman sculptures have some degree of nudity. Sculptors today are back to displaying the beauty of the human body."

That night I had a dream. It started out wonderfully enough. I saw all kinds of white statues, some from Powers' shop, some by other artists, all muscular, beautiful, young. Then the scene shifted to Niagara Falls. I was getting married to a handsome Ojibwe from a neighboring band. Drums beat with joy. My family and many others danced around us. Suddenly, I heard a rumbling cart. Men jumped down from the cart and placed my husband and me in chains. My uncles shot arrows at them but they took us away.

When I awoke the next morning, it all seemed so real. I remembered how my mother and father had told me to listen to my dreams. Lying in bed, it came to me that I would use marble to portray my Negro brothers and sisters who suffered in slavery. The dream told me I could have been one of them.

Then, I would make marble statues of my Ojibwe people who the white man was abusing in another way; forcing them off their land. The "Neoclassical Style," as Powers called it, it would be perfect to give them glory and honor.Mr. Powers knew I was still learning and he let me observe him and his assistants in his studio. He gave me cast-off pieces of marble to practice on.

One day he said, "I came from a family like yours, Edmonia. I know what it is like to struggle to pay for food and a place to live, let alone tools for sculpting. I will give you some of my tools. I have two or three of each."

"I am grateful for any you can spare," I said softly. I remembered what Mr. Brackett had said about people wanting to help me, if I let them.

As happy as I was, I felt lonely. On one of the days I spent admiring Florence's many churches, a young, well-dressed couple stopped in front of me. The woman had her arm around the fellow's waist, and he rested his arm on her shoulder. They put their heads together and pointed to different parts of a church. Then they kissed. At that moment, two women walked up to admire the church. One had graying hair and the other had the sleek black hair of many Italian women. They chatted ever so gaily, arm in arm.

I wondered, "Why not me, God? Why can't I find someone to love?"

When I returned to my room, I asked my otherworldly visitor, "Where are you now that I need you?"

My wooden shutter suddenly blew open and banged against the wall. A cool breeze came in and a female voice whispered, "Roma."

This wasn't exactly the answer I was looking for at that moment, but I said. "So you do approve of my plans."

Wordlessly, the force that blew into my room sucked the cool air right out and closed the shutter. Strangely, it was not the same as the other voice that told me, "You have me, Mary." But it was just as alarming.

After I settled in Powers' shop, I went back to making medallions of American heroes. My heart cried for new subject matter, but Americans making the Grand Tour in Europe bought them with enthusiasm, and I needed the money. Customers talked about how worried they were by the Civil War. When Florentines heard us moan, they mentioned how relieved they had been to finally see the end of their city-states' fighting. It was only three years earlier, in 1861, that their country had been finally unified and given the name "Italy."

During this time, I sculpted a small copy of Michelangelo's Moses, only 26 inches high. That was a challenge, but it turned out well, and I sold it to a wealthy Florentine for his villa.

After the sale, Powers said, "You are ready for Rome, Edmonia. Why don't you join Hosmer and her flock? You will find many American travelers in Rome, and they will love your work."

After Powers sent a letter to Harriet, she wrote back encouraging me to rent a studio down the street from hers.

Rome was a two-day trip from Florence. Looking out the carriage window, I marveled at the rolling hills that formed patterns: squares of grape vines, wheat, olive trees, and horse pastures. The driver said proudly, "This is Tuscany!" On this bright July day, everything looked golden. With dreams of greatness ahead, I hardly felt the bumps of the carriage ride.

When I arrived in Rome, my carriage headed straight for Hosmer's studio. I was struck by the many fountains with Greek and Roman gods spouting water. This is what Powers had taught me was the Classical Style from centuries ago.

We passed the Coliseum. I remembered from my Oberlin history classes that this was where Christians were tortured. Still, the architecture of the building was so impressive. Nearby were ancient buildings with tall marble columns. Most meaningful to me was seeing the Vatican, a city in itself, home to my beloved church.

The carriage took us up a slight hill to Hosmer's studio. With two carpetbags, I stood at the open doorway and took in the scene before me: high ceilings, larger-than-life statues, stepladders, carving tools, and a number of men roughing out marble. But where was Harriet? On a high stepladder in the corner, the queen of sculpting noticed me and climbed down to greet me.

Giving me a handshake so rough and firm that it hurt,

Hosmer said, "Welcome to Rome. My friends and I have so looked forward to your arrival."

Harriet was short and small like me. But, for a little woman, she was very much "in charge." Back in Boston, she had told me of her views about women being equal to men and of her wanting the world to realize that. Although I agreed with her, I found her manner a bit overbearing.

Harriet told me more about the studio she wanted me to take. It had once been the workplace of the great sculptor Antonio Canova, but had sat unused for years.

"With a little clean-up, it will be perfect!" Hosmer sang.

How could I say no?

After she showed me some of her pieces, Harriet took one of my carpetbags in hand and said, "Now, let's go to Canova's place."

In the hot sun, I was sweating like a Roman fountain. After almost two miles, Harriet stopped.

"I have a key for the shop here. The agent who is renting it gave it to me so I could show it to potential renters like you. I hope you like it!"

When Harriet opened the door and I looked around, I had to agree that it looked like a magnificent place to work, with high ceilings and plenty of light and air from its long, slender windows. I had little money left. Again, I would have to write to Samuel.

I sent him a letter in which I raved about all I had seen in Florence and Rome. But, more than his financial help, I longed for his words; words about how he was doing.

Often, he sent money and a quick note wishing me luck, but that was usually all.

After I moved into the studio, Harriet came in—I should say, stormed into—my studio with her usual whirlwind of high intensity.

"Edmonia, my dear, I would like to invite you to the home of Charlotte Cushman. No doubt you heard about her back in America."

"Not really . . ." I began.

"She is America's most famous actress and singer. She has a lovely villa on Via Georgiana. Friday night she is having a party, and I know you will enjoy meeting her along with all of our dear friends."

I went to the party, all dressed up in my gray skirt, frilly white blouse, and a new imitation pearl necklace.

A servant showed me into the villa. Its walls were painted from floor to ceiling with scenes of Roman life. In the middle of the main room was a fountain. Next to the fountain, Miss Cushman sat in her large, red velvet chair, speaking loudly to six or seven women. They listened in silence. She was not my idea of a famous actress. Cushman was rather homely and spoke in a gravelly voice. Her attire and that of the other women was not very feminine. They wore long dark skirts, white blouses, ties, and berets. Not a hint of jewelry.

When she saw me, Miss Cushman stood and said, "Come, sit with us, Miss Lewis. We have been waiting for you." I thought, Of course, she knows who I am, the only brown-skinned woman here.

I sat upon a blue velvet chair, and the women turned their attention to me.

"It's good to see you again," said Anne Whitney, a sculptor I had met back in Boston.

Ever so politely, the women asked questions about my background and praised me for what they heard I had accomplished. Like it was some kind of miracle that a young woman of my heritage could do anything of merit. It brought back memories of Miss Child. When I returned to my studio home that night, I knew I would have trouble sleeping. After slipping into a nightgown, I lit a candle and walked into my studio. I sat down next to a two-foot high piece of marble that I had planned to begin sculpting the next day.

It was like sitting with my rock back at the Falls. I couldn't write on this piece of stone, but I could talk to it. "They're all so nice to me. Is it only because of the color of my skin?"

Just like my rock, the marble didn't answer, but at least it listened.

∽◌∾

I couldn't wait to get back to my sculpting. Ever since my dream back in Florence, I knew I would sculpt my subjects with nobility. I was always searching for new inspiration. I decided to go to St. Peter's. I so looked forward to seeing the home of the Pope. During my two-mile walk, I admired a number of beautiful, old Catholic churches as well as ruins of ancient Roman buildings.

When I arrived outside St. Peter's, I was struck by its gigantic piazza and then by the cathedral's tall doors. Entering the basilica, I saw two oversized sets of angelic-looking naked children. I later learned they were "cherubs." Each marble pair held a shallow bowl of holy water. Quietly, I said hello to the frozen little angels and then touched some water to my forehead. After I blessed myself, I stared down the long aisle lined by tall, fancy columns. I walked toward the huge brown altar with all kinds of carvings. Behind it was a stained glass window, bursting with golden sunbeams, clouds, and angels.

I sat in awe for a while, and then left to explore the rest of the Vatican.

I had no idea the Vatican held a huge museum. How had the Church collected all this art? I especially loved the hanging carpets depicting scenes from the Bible. On one rug, Jesus' eyes seemed to follow me as I walked.

When I went outside, it was pleasing to stroll through the piazza. To rest my legs, I sat at the base of one of the large columns.

I had been so busy since leaving Oberlin that I hadn't had a chance to think. I tried to push my bad memories aside, but I was haunted by visions of Mrs. Dascomb commanding me to leave and of the boys beating me. I still hated the boys and the headmistress, but I knew this anger held me back, and hurt my soul.

As I sat thinking of how I could get past it, I spotted a young white fellow with blonde hair. His head was down as he sat reading a book. He happened to look up in my direction and smiled. I looked away and headed home.

Trying to cleanse my damaged soul, I returned a couple of times a week to the Vatican to look at its art and stroll around the piazza. I often saw the blonde boy. When he smiled at me, I finally smiled back. But I gave him very little thought.

⁓◯⁓

At least once a week, I joined the others at Charlotte Cushman's villa. I found out that her manly appearance was of benefit in her acting career, because she often played men. She explained that in the States few men became actors, because it wasn't considered a serious occupation.

Once, when I arrived early, and it was just Miss Cushman and me, she asked, "What are you planning to sculpt next, Edmonia?"

"I don't know."

"What speaks to you? What's in your soul crying to get out?"

"I think a great deal about injustice, about oppressed people."

"Such as?"

"My mother's people, the Ojibwe Indians in New York and Canada. I think of my colored brothers and sisters in chains, women not given the chances men have."

"Well, then that's what you should make," said Charlotte, with a knowing smile.

"I'll tell you what. If you come to me with ideas for a sculpture that has to do with injustice, I will pay for the marble."

I was shocked. "Really?"

I was quiet that night; I couldn't stop thinking about Charlotte's offer. When I got home, I thought about what I would sculpt.

I decided it would be a bust of an Ojibwe woman. In fact, the face of Mineehaha from Longfellow's poem about Hiawatha. Yes, that would be my first sculpture of my people. So many thought of us Indians as violent savages. Mineehaha would be gentle and sweet.

I arrived early for the next gathering, to share my idea with Charlotte. She was more than happy to pay for the marble. With all my heart I thanked her, but went on about it too long, because when the others came, they asked what the two of us had been talking about. Charlotte was unapologetic about paying for my project, but I didn't know how the others would take it.

It was 1865. We Americans in Rome celebrated with joy when we heard the Union had finally won the bloody conflict. With all my heart, I thanked Jesus, the Great Spirit, and my father's Supreme Being.

This victory inspired me to make a marble statue of a colored man and woman breaking free from their chains. When visitors to my shop looked at it, I heard whispers, "They don't look negro."

I explained that I had given them the classical features of the ancient Greeks and Romans. I'm not sure they understood.

I followed through on my wish to sculpt my other oppressed brothers and sisters and cast them in a noble light–an Ojibwe couple getting married in elegant beauty, and busts of other Ojibwe characters from Longfellow's poem. Then I carved a life-size statue of Hagar, the servant mother of one of Abraham's sons. Abraham had treated her so unfairly, throwing her into the wilderness after his aged wife had finally given him a son.

Making the statues and selling them were two different things. I didn't wait for commissions, like everyone else in my profession did. I made statues and shipped them back to America. I asked my abolitionist friends to sell them. It took them a long time to find buyers.

When I mentioned this to one of the other sculptors, she asked, "Don't you think you're being a little pushy?' I heard another say under her breath, "What nerve."

I didn't care if the ladies thought I had a strange way of selling my art. When I felt inspired to make a statue, I didn't wait around for someone to order it.

Selling took courage. From the time I was a little girl sewing my beadwork, I knew how to get people to buy my art. Now I was taking advantage of my workshop being down the street from one of our most famous American sculptors, William Story. Many people came to view his work and then stopped by my studio. Like other sculptors, I left my door open. I smiled at passersby in a way that welcomed them to come and watch me work. Their sighs and murmurs told me they were amazed that I—a colored woman—could be capable of such creativity. But, as long as they bought my art, I didn't care what they thought.

Among the Cushman crowd, I felt most comfortable with Charlotte. The other sculptors surprised me by the familiar way they touched each other, more like men and women would. They even exchanged kisses, though only on the cheek.

One evening a sculptor named Elisabeth asked, "Edmonia, come with me for a moment? I need to talk with you alone."

When we entered the room, Elisabeth put her hand on my shoulder and her face close to mine. "Do you know you are very pretty?"

"Uh, no," I stammered.

"You lack confidence, Edmonia. I could help you feel better about yourself." At that, Elisabeth stroked my hair. Then she kissed me softly on the cheek, for more than just a moment.

I didn't know if I liked it or not.

At that moment, Charlotte called us together. "I want to know what everyone thought of Story's latest exhibition."

Elisabeth took my elbow and led me into the room as if she was my beau.

After the meeting was over, I just about ran from the place. Elisabeth stared at me strangely as I said goodbye. When I got home, I lay on my bed. What just happened? Did a woman want me, as if she were a man? Did I ask for this attention? Do I like other women like that?

After the beating at Oberlin, it was still hard for me to trust men. Perhaps it would be safer to be with a woman. I grabbed for my Chianti and probably drank more that should have.

I buried myself in my work and didn't return to Cushman's the next Friday. I needed time.

One of the projects I got busy with had to do with Henry Wadsworth Longfellow. Like many well-to-do American writers, he spent months each year visiting Rome. One of the sculptors in our group talked about how she had him pose for a bust.

When I asked her to tell me when he was coming to her studio, so I could meet him, she laughed and said, "I don't like anyone around when I sculpt."

I thought; His poem inspired the sculptures of my Indian subjects. If I can't meet him, I will do what I did with Colonel Shaw. I'll observe him, and sketch him.

Longfellow occasionally took a morning stroll past my shop. As I worked on a small statue of Mary, I kept one eye on the street. Once I got used to his routine, I went outside and sketched him.

Working from my drawings and a picture of him in the newspaper, I started sculpting his head. After a month, it was almost complete. I was going to ask him to look at it, until one day a gentleman signed my guestbook with the name, "Sam Longfellow."

"Are you related to Henry Wadsworth Longfellow?"

"You might say that. He happens to be my brother."

"Can I show you something?"

I led him to a corner of my studio and pointed to the marble.

"Oh, my goodness!" he exclaimed. "That's my brother."

He later brought Henry to look at the bust. Longfellow

said, "There's another bust that a sculptor was working on. It doesn't resemble me. Instead of paying her, I'd rather buy this one."

The next time I showed up at Cushman's regular Friday night get-together, I was a little shaky. I was afraid that Elisabeth would approach me again. I still didn't know how I felt about that. I didn't have to worry, though, because the group gave me the cold shoulder. The sculptor who did the bust of Longfellow shot me a look. She must have told the other women what I had done. I realized they would never invite me again.

This rejection was my fault. It may have saved me from making a decision about Elisabeth's advances, but I regretted that I lost the only friends I had in Rome. The Cushman ladies would never forgive me, and I couldn't forgive myself.

I returned home that night, sat in my chair, and held my head in my hands. I had never been so angry with myself. I threw a pot at the wall. I wanted to tear the place apart. I yelled at myself, "Stupid, stupid, stupid!"

Ever since I lost my parents, I just wanted to fit in. I had ruined yet another chance for friendship.

It was sweltering outside, so I had my back door open. I was sitting at my kitchen table, staring at my food. Suddenly, a cool breeze blew in, and a white filmy substance shot through the open door. I tilted back and almost toppled over. The white film took the form of the woman on a throne, the same one I had seen at the Keeps' house!

The woman said in a wavy voice to match her wavy

172

substance, "I made a mistake once for which I couldn't forgive myself. Don't quit, though, like I did. This pain will pass."

She didn't just leave abruptly like she did at the Keeps': she undulated around my kitchen several times. Her final words were, "Carve my likeness."

At that, she dissolved into a thin cloud and floated out the doorway, taking the coolness with her.

Needless to say, I was overwhelmed, and confused. This figure's voice was a deep one, like the one that had said, "Roma."

~∞~

I hardly slept that night. Every time I heard a creak, I flinched.

The next day, I hurried to the Vatican. I paced around the piazza. Then I saw the blonde boy, reading again. He closed his book and was getting up as if ready to go. He wore a white shirt with brown suspenders that he probably needed, because he was on the thin side. He walked up to me. I didn't know what to expect.

"Don't you love this spot? I see you come here as often as I do."

Getting a close look at him, I could see his blue eyes shone with the same optimism as Samuel's brown ones. After a few seconds, I stammered, "Oh, yes. It's a fine place to think."

He smiled and extended his hand. "My name is Peter. It's good to meet another American thinker." He didn't ask my name but said he hoped to see me again.

This certainly took my mind off the falling out with my friends, and my most recent visitation.

As much as I didn't trust men, especially white fellows, I visited the Vatican daily, hoping to see Peter. One day, I was strolling through the piazza when suddenly Peter was walking at my side. I told him my name. He said I was the first "Edmonia" he had ever met. We talked about where we grew up. His childhood was much more "normal' than mine. When I told him of life with my mother's people, he had so many questions. Finally, I wasn't alone with my thoughts anymore.

Peter was from a wealthy family in Boston. He was in Rome working on his doctorate in art history. Within six weeks, he would be finished with his studies and heading back to New York to become a professor.

I liked him and I thought he liked me. Then I got scared. I was afraid he would hurt me. I avoided the Vatican and went to the Spanish Steps instead. It wasn't fun, like being with Peter, but at least I lost that feeling of fear.

One day, as I was walking down the Steps, there was Peter at the bottom. He said that he had gone to a different tourist spot every day looking for me. At that moment, I was sure I had finally found a man who liked me, someone I could trust.

We started meeting at the Steps almost every day. On a sunny morning that made Rome's marble look brighter and whiter than ever, Peter looked closely at me. I had hardly slept the night before. He touched my chin and asked, "What's wrong?"

It took me a while, but I finally told him about the

Oberlin boys and how I had had a nightmare about them the night before. "I just can't get the one with yellow eyes out of my mind."

"I wish I could have been there, to protect you."

"And now it's hard for me to trust whites."

"Don't let this this anger control you, Edmonia. That was just one group of boys. Don't judge all of us."

I felt one of my walls come down.

"Now I know why you quit coming to the piazza," he said.

Peter and I went out to eat and explore Rome together. Sometimes we would hold hands. One day, when we sat down at a street café, I decided to trust him enough to tell him my other secret. I pretended it only involved dreams. I didn't want him to think I was crazy.

Peter sat back and said, "So, in your dreams you see a woman on a throne and she wants you to carve her likeness?"

"Right, on both counts. I feel she is a queen, but I don't know who she is. My only clue is she wears a big headdress. It looks like a raven or some other large bird."

"She must be Egyptian. Pharaohs wore bird headdresses. There were only two queen pharaohs. One was Hatshepsut. I've studied statues of her, but she didn't wear a headdress."

"You learned all this in your art history classes?"

Peter laughed. "Yes, and it's nice to put my knowledge to work for a change."

"Who was the other Egyptian queen?"

"Cleopatra."

"Cleopatra! That woman—Cleopatra! Back in Boston people put on plays showing her as a wild, wicked woman."

"Right or not, she did get a reputation for being rather licentious, Peter said. "But she accomplished so much, more than any woman of her time. She loved Egypt."

"Ah yes, she's from Africa, the home of my father's people. That is, before the French took them to Haiti in chains."

"A terrible part of world history," Peter scowled.

I was silent, then said, "I hate to admit it, but sometimes I'm ashamed that I am part Negro."

With a look of shock, Peter asked, "Why?"

"When people look at me, they may think of me as a slave."

Now Peter was silent for a while.

"It makes me feel . . . like I'm beneath them."

Peter became passionate. "But your ancestors, they were kidnapped from Africa. It took courage to survive all they suffered. You should be proud."

I felt another of my walls coming down.

Peter continued, thoughtfully, "Cleopatra is the one speaking to you in your dreams. She wouldn't want you to feel ashamed. She chose you as her sculptor, because of your talent and your roots in Africa. Don't you see, this is an honor?"

I stared out in space for a while. "I have so much to think about."

"Don't think." He touched my lips. "Smile."

Three weeks later, it was time for Peter to return to the States. On a balmy late Friday afternoon, I walked with him to the dock, where his ship waited. Peter hugged me, pulled me close, and gave me a long, deep kiss.

The only verse I remembered from Longfellow's poem came back to me:

Thus departed Hiawatha,
Hiawatha, the Beloved,
In the glory of the sunset,
In the purple mist of evening

To the regions of the home-wind
To the Land of the Hereafter.

After the long kiss, I didn't think about Elisabeth's advances again. Unlike the women in the Cushman group, I had been attracted to a man. I would leave it at that.

The next morning, I woke in a daze and returned to my regular routine. I put on my work clothes and returned to chiseling a cherub for a wealthy American patron, but I couldn't concentrate. I wasn't angry with Peter that he had left, but I was sad. He had warned me his time in Rome would be short. And he never said he was "in love" with me.

As I tried to work, I heard a loud pounding at my workshop door. When I opened it, a sweaty, tired-looking man said, "We have your marble."

I had ordered this marble two months earlier when, without my asking, Samuel surprised me with a large amount of money. I didn't know what I would do with the marble then, but now I knew.

PART EIGHT
CREATION

The Statue
1872

WHEN THE BELLA SPOSA REACHED Ostia, it looked like a ghost town. The port city was once a colony of Rome and featured the first Forum. At one time, it had had fountains, columned buildings, and lifelike statues; however, when the Roman Empire collapsed, pirates looted its greatest sculptures and artifacts.

But there were still some old marble statues in Ostia, standing in the ancient ruins of the market square and decorating temples to the gods. They showed how beauty could be fashioned from flesh like mine. They looked like real people, frozen in position. Some were standing, some reclined. Some were clothed, others revealed the beauty of the human body.

The bustling harbor of Ostia was not as glorious as the La Spieza harbor. It was narrow and shallow, clogged with silt carried down the Tiber.

When we finally made it up the Tiber to Rome, there was marble flesh like mine everywhere on display. It fashioned gurgling fountains that delighted the eye and ear. The Roman citizens filled their vessels in these fountains with fresh water, from the mountains, that rushed down their massive aqueducts. There were grand temples, huge statues, ornate columns, gigantic arches, and towering obelisks.

They transported me by horse-drawn wagon to a low, whitewashed building. There was nothing on the outside to indicate what was inside. The men who drove my wagon hoisted me with a device called a gantry. The ancient Greeks had invented it. If you consider it could lift 10,000 pounds, I wasn't that heavy.

When the men knocked, a young woman threw open the wooden door and signed a paper. She pointed to where they should place me. I passed through wide doors into a large workshop. The woman directed the men to place me upright atop a four-foot high wooden pedestal. I sat tall, not knowing what the young woman would do with me. I hoped she would make me into something lovely.

The workshop, where I sat on my pedestal, had a high ceiling, with heavy beams supporting the roof. Long slender windows ushered in light that illuminated objects in the room: ladders, metal tools, and other pieces of marble poised on pedestals. Some were starting to look human.

The young woman came to me. I had known her since she was a young girl running carefree through the forest. She was short and slender. Her buttery complexion was a soft brown. She wore a red hat, with a golden tassel hanging down. She also wore rough work clothes and a heavy smock. On her hands were thick leather gloves. These belied her delicate features. She had deep brown eyes. Her lips were full and her black curly hair fell into soft ringlets.

Most beautiful of all was the warmth in her eyes as she gazed at me. I could tell she was attracted to me as she removed her glove and passed her bare hand over my smooth surface. She looked at me from all sides and couldn't suppress a smile. She patted me and said a word softly with a charming accent: "Jiibay."

Finally, someone cared about me, unlike those characters who brought me here, starting with the cavatori, who had cursed my stubbornness. They handled me so roughly. I was only a problem to them. Whenever it was time for workers to move me, they cursed and spat. There was relief on their faces when they were through with me.

But here was a woman who wanted me. She had sent for me, and paid for me to be transported almost 200 miles. I had no idea what she would do, but I yearned for her to create my majestic likeness; a statue where my ka could finally find rest. I didn't know what shape that would take but knew she would make me beautiful. I didn't realize she had much work to do even before she started changing me.

Edmonia Lewis
Twenty-Eight to Thirty-Two Years Old
1872-1876

AFTER THE DELIVERY MEN LEFT, I stood there and stared at the slab. Even though the weather was warm, a, cool sensation radiated from my head to my toes. I didn't want it to stop. I touched the marble, and it was cool. I stepped back. The sensation stopped. When I got close to the marble again, the feeling returned, although only for a few seconds.

It reminded me of how I felt when, as a girl I would run through the forest to a hill where I would look down at the Falls, hear the roar, and watch the graceful eagles glide up and down through the blue sky. Waves of ecstasy went through my body as I ran back home. I felt I could run forever.

I just stood there, admiring the stone. Unlike some of my marble that had dark veins, this gigantic piece was almost pure white. I touched it again and admired its beauty. I heard myself say, "Jiibay (ghost)."

Then I said, "Stay right here." I laughed at myself and added, "I guess you won't be going anywhere."

Rushing out of my workshop, I hailed a carriage to take me to the Vatican.

Arriving at the museum, I hurried up the stairs. I knew where the Egyptian exhibit was and I had talked to its curator.

I rushed into the woman's office and found her sitting there going through some papers.

"Buon giorno," I said.

"Buon giorno to you. We have spoken before, I believe."

"Yes, I am Edmonia Lewis. You can call me Edmonia."

"I remember. I am Mrs. Massri. Can I help you?"

"I would like to sculpt a statue of Queen Cleopatra, sitting on a throne. I don't see any statues of pharaohs on thrones here."

"We have a limited collection. It was very popular to sculpt the pharaohs standing straight, looking very noble, like what we have here. But some showed them sitting on thrones."

"I'm glad to hear that," I sighed, with too much feeling. Mrs. Massri stared at me.

Then she said, "I have art history books that show how the Egyptian artisans sculpted the sitting pharaohs. Through the centuries, they used a similar style." She explained how the sculptor drew front and side views on the faces of a rectangular block and then worked inward until these views met.

"I'd like to look at those books."

Mrs. Massri explained how each pharaoh had a ka, or spirit. If a suitable statue was made after the pharaoh's death, the ka would make its home in the statue. But if the statue wasn't what he wanted, the pharaoh's ka would wander until it found the right artist to capture their essence.

I could hardly breathe. This explained everything.

She asked, "Are you all right?"

"Yes, yes," I pretended. I was in shock but felt that somehow I knew all along this was what I was meant to do.

"You are welcome to borrow these." Mrs. Massri lifted two heavy books from her collection. "These describe the exact process." Then she picked out one more book. "Also, here is the story of Cleopatra's life, if you need to know a little more about her history."

In a rare burst of emotion, I hugged her. She looked uncomfortable.

"One more thing, Miss Lewis, we have a collection of coins showing Cleopatra's face. They were minted during her reign." She pointed to a glass-covered display. "They may help you."

"Thank you, Mrs. Massri, I'll be careful with your books."

She smiled, "I trust you. Are you sure you're all right, Edmonia?"

I knew I had been trembling. "I guess the heat just got to me."

As I was leaving, Mrs. Massri added, "By the way, you'll need a model; I can recommend an agent right down the street."

Having done most of my work from quick observations and grainy newspaper photos, I hadn't thought about hiring a model. After she gave me directions, I rushed to the agency.

I arranged for a model to arrive at my workshop the next day. However, overwhelmed by all of Mrs. Massri's talk of ka, I still had one place left to go—the workshop of William Story.

"Ah, my competitor, little Edmonia Lewis, who steals my customers," he said.

I acted innocent. "What do you mean?"

"Come on. You love having your workshop near mine. After people look at my works, it's only a short walk to where the little colored sculptor creates amazing sculptures, without assistants."

"I have to work alone. If I had help, my assistants would get all the credit. It's because I'm colored . . . well, you know."

Story softened. "Yes, you do have a predicament there . . ." his voice trailed off.

Then, brightening up, he asked, "What can I do for you?"

"I would like to see your statue of the Death of Cleopatra. I admire it so."

Never tired of showing his favorite sculpture, he pointed to the statue displayed on a fancy pedestal at the back of his studio. "It will be a pleasure, as long as you don't steal my ideas."

"Never," I lied.

Having seen the statue at one of his open houses, I again studied his version of Cleopatra at her death. The technical skill of the carving was magnificent. He had captured the folds of her robe, the features of her face, and polished it to a shiny patina. Story's Cleopatra looked serious, but she looked like she could have been considering what to wear that night. She looked so perfect. And she looked too Greek or Roman. Her chair could have been in one of Rome's aristocratic homes. It was open in the back, with only one skinny backrest. It was nothing like a throne. Story depicted Cleopatra's hands, feet, and face realistically, and he also showed both her breasts without covering.

I complimented Mr. Story on his fine piece and left.

When I got back to my workshop, I opened the door with quivering hands. The other-worldliness of the marble scared me.

After taking off my shawl, I went directly to my back room and started reading. I learned that when Egyptian artists sculpted a pharaoh on a throne there were no separations between the stone and the body. The pharaoh and the stone were one. This showed he was a permanent being that would last forever, like a rock. This kind of throne would keep his or her ka safe. He would always exist on earth and the after-life. I learned, too, about symbols used on a pharaoh's throne, like animals' heads and lotus plants. A falcon would be on his head with wings on each side to keep him safe. I began reading the book about Cleopatra's life. I learned so much more about the queen and all the triumphant as well as terrible events in her life. Unbelieveable! It was so sad that, as a young child, she was exposed to all the killing in her family, and it was tragic that she had to let go of her children at the end. She would have been separated from them anyhow if she were made a slave, or worse.

Then I got up my courage to return to the marble.

I stood right in front of it and felt again its cool effect! I touched it, and, just like before, it was cold.

I said, "You have been working on me since I was a child. Now, it's time for me to get to work. I will make you so magnificent, a statue the whole world will admire!"

The marble's cool effect relaxed me. I thought some more. Then I added, "You will be noble in death. You took your life rather than live like a slave. I will show that final look on your face, of resignation. Because you felt no choice but to kill yourself."

I told the marble of the ads for circus sideshows I had seen in Boston. The posters showed the queen as a woman who tempted men. They even made her death strangely exciting.

No reaction.

I continued to speak boldly. "I know now that you were the one who came to me in my darkest hour and said, 'Don't give up, like I did.' That makes you a kinder woman than people give you credit for. I want to show your human side."

The cool draft returned.

It took time for me to form my thoughts and put them into words. "When you appeared to me on your throne, you wore a long, thin, tight dress. Looking at Mrs. Massri's books, I see that's how Egyptian royalty dressed. I will change that. You will have long flowing robes."

The coolness left. I thought maybe she wasn't pleased with that.

"That's because I will sculpt you in the neoclassical style. It's the latest thing, a big hit with people now. Artists go back to ancient styles and show their subjects in robes like the Greeks and Romans wore. If it's any comfort, they only choose the most notable individuals. Along with the neoclassical style comes an appreciation of the human body. I will sculpt you, as most of our artists in Rome do, with your breast exposed, possibly to accept the asp."

A slight coolness returned.

I thought some more. "But your sculpture will be different, because you were Egyptian and because of your final look. I will make your throne look like a real Egyptian throne, with a nineteenth century twist. You will be one with the stone like ancient pharaohs were. You will be admired forever. Your ka will finally rest."

Lots of coolness radiated towards me.

"But, remember, this sculpture will be different too, because it will show that you were human, with your head flung back in resignation."

I guess Cleopatra was considering this. No matter what she thought, I would go ahead with my plans.

Cleopatra

NOW THAT THE MARBLE WAS safely ensconced in Edmonia's workshop, I met the young woman who would pose for my statue. I must say she was a good choice. She radiated my superior air but also had much in common with my creator and me. We had been wild in our youth: petty thieves, no less.

She had a slightly olive complexion, like my mother. She had a strong nose and sturdy chin, like my baba. Dark curls framed her face. Her body was well developed and not completely covered. She reclined on a high-back chair for hours. There was a blank expression in her dark eyes, and she barely spoke. She sat in the same pose, her face twisted toward my statue's creator, her long left arm dangling from the chair.

Her name was Allegra Salvi, and she had just turned 18. Her family lived in the Prati neighborhood, across from the Vatican. They had a handsome apartment. Allegra's bedroom was like a suite. It even had a balcony, where she stood, sneaking cigarettes, while gazing at the walls of the Pope's holy kingdom.

Thanks to her mother's taste in decoration, the apartment would have looked right at home in the Vatican. Statues and portraits of saints cluttered the rooms. Her mother, Angela, blessed herself with water consecrated by the Pope when she entered the apartment.

The Statue

MY SCULPTOR WALKED TO ALLEGRA and showed her how she wanted her to arch her spine and toss her head back. This made the model instantly uncomfortable. As Allegra turned her face toward my creator, annoyance spread from her eyes and distorted her delicate features.

Allegra attended an all-girls school, as was the custom. Her parents prayed for her to find her vocation as a nun. After being taught by these stern women in their starched gowns, Allegra wanted no part of it. When the school bell sounded, she sprang down the steps to explore her lovely neighborhood.

Prati was quiet and clean, far from the turmoil of central Rome. It was dotted with public squares that had trim lawns and sculpted gardens. Elegant buildings lined the streets, along with lively cafes. Allegra's favorite place was along the banks of the Tiber, where stylish restaurants overlooked the water. At one of these, her friend Carlo worked as a dishwasher.

As Allegra thought of him, her face relaxed into the blank expression my sculptor wanted. She couldn't help wondering if her aquiline nose would bear any resemblance to the Egyptian queen. How could her strong Italian features possibly pass for a woman who was half Greek?

As she sat, Allegra sank into a daydream. She would wait for Carlo to get off work and they would invade the neighborhood. They were literally partners in crime, snatching valuables from the high-end shops along the Via Cola di Riendo. Once, she was walking out of one of these shops with an expensive scarf stuffed in her pocket. Carlo had stolen his own treasure, a small gilded crucifix.

My sculptor came over, lifted Allegra's right arm, and rested it on her thigh. She opened the fingers of her right hand, to accept the serpent. Then she pushed the model's right leg back toward the chair. This made Allegra unsteady, and she felt like she might slide right off the chair.

When Allegra and Carlo emerged from the shop, she didn't know if it was their guilty looks that had given them away, or the small piece of scarf sticking out of her pocket. Like my creator, she was caught committing a crime.

The shop owner angrily confronted them on the sidewalk. He retrieved his merchandise and hailed a policeman. The polizia marched Allegra to her home and told her mother what she had been up to and with whom.

Angela was mortified, mostly because Carlo had

stolen the crucifix. She forbade Allegra to associate with a low-class thief, and commanded that she come home immediately from school. That night, Allegra packed a small case and hid it in a bush in front of the apartment. The next morning, she dutifully put on her school uniform. But, once outside, she grabbed her case and raced to the riverbank.

My creator stopped her work with the clay to pull Allegra's left foot forward, which made her feel a bit more secure on her "throne." She asked Allegra to relax her left arm. Allegra complied. But, when she had Allegra push her hips forward, the model once again felt like she was going to slither onto the floor.

Allegra found Carlo at work and convinced him that they both needed to leave home and find a room somewhere. They moved in with one of the cooks, who didn't ask questions but gladly took their money. Allegra had broken free from her mother's grip and searched for work.

She saw a studio that was hiring models and bounded up the stairs. In a drab office, a questionable looking man offered her a good deal of money to pose for statues and paintings. He ran an agency that supplied models to local artists. Most of them came from very poor families and supplemented their income with prostitution. Allegra wouldn't think of that. Posing nude was deliciously wicked enough to outrage her sainted mother. However, by the time she met me, she had learned how boring sin could be.

Because of the position she was in, Allegra's stomach swelled beneath the simple cord that kept her purple robe closed. She thought this made her even less attractive and this fueled her increasing anger toward this demanding little woman and her absurd commands.

My sculptor adjusted the elaborate covering on Allegra's head. The model wore bracelets and she liked the delicate sandals the sculptor had picked out. She reclined there motionless. She looked annoyed whenever my creator gave her another command. Allegra would change her position almost imperceptibly and settle back into boredom.

My creator stood at a table, with her eyes fixed on the reclining figure. As she stared, her hands worked a soft substance that had a light orange hue. Her fingers moved independently, as they knew just what to do. My sculptor didn't look down while she replicated the features of the young woman in the chair.

This process went on for many days. Allegra sighed each time she had to sit. She didn't look at me and kept her eyes free of all expression. It was pitiful how sitting was stifling her spirit. She never smiled. Her sighs increased the longer she sat. She had escaped the tyranny of her mother, only to be under the thumb of this impossible woman

One afternoon, she could take no more of keeping the unbearable pose. She stood up suddenly and demanded to take a break. She rubbed her backside. It had gone numb from keeping her position. With modesty a distant memory, she did not attempt to close her robe.

"What is this monster you're creating," she asked. "My boss told me you were creating Cleopatra, but this is grotesque." There was fire in Allegra's eyes.

"I should be sitting upright on the throne, like a queen. Instead, you have me in the most undignified position. It's torture."

My sculptor gave no answer to this outburst.

"Tell me, artist, what rich Roman paid you to make this? And where would they put it? There's no way it could fit through our door, and I know the Vatican would never allow this abomination.

"If you wanted ugliness, why did you hire me? My face and body can be seen in masterpieces. I am chosen for my beauty, but you make me feel ugly."

Instead of responding to Allegra, my sculptor asked her to resume her pose. The model reluctantly reclined on the high-back chair. The short brown woman walked over to make small adjustments to her position. She placed a pillow behind her to increase the arch of her back. She asked Allegro to relax her mouth to allow her lips to part slightly.

As Allegra twisted her face to gaze at my sculptor, her expression had hardened into a certain haughtiness. This offset Allegra's graceful neck and her supple body. It was the perfect look for a dying queen.

Allegra posed for several more days, until my creator captured her in clay. There was Allegra in miniature form! My sculptor had captured every fold of her robe, every feature of her face. No detail had escaped her searching eyes. Although she portrayed the young woman's outward beauty, there was no hint of her troubled soul.

Allegra rose from the chair and gasped at what she saw. The likeness was far from pretty, but it possessed a terrible beauty. It was not the form of a wild teenager but of a mature woman of substance. The clay figure radiated the power, wisdom, and strength of a woman who had died by her own hand. Allegra couldn't wait to tell Carlo she was finished with the job. He was so tired of hearing her complain.

PART NINE
DISPLAY

The Statue

THE YOUNG MODEL WAS GONE forever but her likeness began to emerge in my stone. I did not know it would take my sculptor four years to capture my spirit. She worked on other statues during this time: small, intricately carved figures. I was the giant of the workshop. I didn't mind when my sculptor pounded her chisel to remove my excess flesh. Her hard work and attention to detail just made me feel more loved.

When I was finished, I faced a long sea journey to a young land that was preparing to celebrate its first important birthday. When I arrived in this country's birthplace, I was so proud of my beauty. I couldn't wait for people to see me.

My wagon brought me to a stately building. Like me, it was new. In front were two enormous bronze statues of winged Pegasus, the grandest of all steeds. Famous figures from the ancient world soothed the horses. Erato, the muse of romantic verse, sang to her horse, while Calliope, the muse of language, told her horse a story.

The horses guarded the entrance to Memorial Hall. Atop the building were four large figures, representing the spirit of the young country: Industry, Commerce, Agriculture, and Navigation. As for the last one, the young country had sent a ship for me to cross the sea.

Perched proudly on top of Memorial Hall was the young country's goddess, Columbia, gazing out over the city. The exterior of the building was granite, a stone that is almost immortal.

Inside the museum, ornate plasterwork covered the walls. It was a fitting place for royalty, a spot where people could admire my majesty. The Centennial Exposition, as the birthday celebration was called, was a national sensation. Almost 10 million people came to see wonders like me during the six months I sat there.

They not only came to gaze at the queen, they spoke of me excitedly. Of the 673 sculptures in that place, I was the talk of the entire exhibit. It's true, not all were enamored. For some reason, people the same color as my sculptor shunned me. At the end of the exposition, judges awarded sculptors for their work. They handed out 43 Awards of Excellence but somehow my sculptor received none. I was stunned. Could they not see my beauty?

As my sculptor promised, I was finally on display for the world to see, and people were impressed! Regardless of whether they liked my dramatic pose, they couldn't look away. That was enough for me.

Edmonia Lewis

WHEN I WAS IN PHILADELPHIA, I wrote two letters: one to my brother, and one to my relatives at Niagara. I invited them to the Centennial to see my work. I said I would pay for their transportation. It had been 19 years since I had seen Samuel and 17 years since I had seen the rest. I hoped they would come but by the time I sealed the letters, I knew they wouldn't.

My legs were tired from standing each day at the exhibition, but I enjoyed talking with the spectators. One gentleman approached me and said that he had read in a newspaper that I went to Oberlin College. In fact, his son was in my class, but I did not recognize the name. He added that the Oberlin Review (the college's newspaper) followed my career and wrote about my many accomplishments.

This discussion showed me how I would satisfy my Ojibwe need for revenge. I wrote a letter to Mrs. Dascomb and enclosed one of my fancy calling cards with my picture on it.

Dear Miss Dascomb,

Please accept my invitation to come to the Centennial Exposition in Philadelphia to see my fine marble statues. It is unfortunate you expelled me. Now, Oberlin College cannot claim me as a member of the alumni.

Mary Edmonia Lewis

I felt good when I mailed it, and I didn't waste any more energy over my old headmistress.

Within a few weeks, I read reviews of my work by the art critics. The first was by J.S. Ingram, who wrote in his Centennial Exposition that the most remarkable piece of sculpture in the American exhibit was The Death of Cleopatra.

Another critic, Walter J. Clark, said that the striking qualities of the work were undeniable, and only a sculptor of genuine endowments could have produced such a statue. However, Clark said that the effects of death were represented with such skill as to be absolutely repellent. When I read his review, I was elated at first but then found out that most newspapers only quoted the words "absolutely repellent."

Every day when I came to Cleopatra, I greeted her in a most cheerful manner. I patted her, and she sent me her comforting coolness.

One day a group of colored people, dressed in black suits and white dresses, walked up to my statue and me. They said, "Hello," and some shook my hand. Then they started pointing at Cleopatra, whispering to each other and frowning.

Two evenings later, I read an article that one of them submitted to The Philadelphia Times. It said their group was from Philadelphia's AME (African Methodist Episcopal) Church, the largest in the city, and that they found the nakedness of The Death of Cleopatra "embarrassing."

Why was it all right for a white man to show the female body, but not a colored woman?

The next morning, when I saw Cleopatra, I felt a little sad. However, almost everyone that day complimented my work. A Negro man introduced himself as John P. Sampson. We chatted about the statue. He was a tall, very dark-skinned gentleman with a full beard and a full smile to match. Mr. Sampson was a university professor and an AME minister.

"I admire your Cleopatra, Miss Lewis. It's so real, a magnificent work of art!"

I felt myself blushing. "It's quite different, don't you

think? I mean, from other sculptures of today, especially in America"

"I've studied art and often attend exhibitions, and I comment on them. I'm refreshed by your originality, your honest rendition of death."

"Thank you, sir. It is so nice to hear that you appreciate my Cleopatra." I felt comfortable with this man. It was a lonely job, standing by my statue all day.

I didn't want him to leave, so I asked if he'd like to see some of my other pieces.

He nodded.

I whispered to Cleopatra, "Be back soon."

Reverend Sampson laughed. "Now you're talking to her?"

If only he knew.

I told him I was sad that my own people . . . instead of encouraging me, they criticized. "After all I've done," I complained. I told him about my statue Forever Free, glorifying a colored man and woman finally breaking the bonds of slavery.

I don't know what it was about the reverend's manner that made me share so much. Maybe it was the way he looked and listened so intently.

Then a thought came out that I didn't know was in my heart. "I don't think I'll return to America after this visit. I just don't feel comfortable here."

A week later, I read a review of The Death of Cleopatra that Mr. Sampson published in The Christian Recorder. He praised Cleopatra as a "magnificent work of art." He described me as "a downright sensible person .

. . of no foolishness, a devoted lover of her race." The morning after reading that review, I greeted Cleopatra with something like joy.

The Centennial was not a place to sell one's work, but I hoped and prayed that someone would offer to buy my queen.

How would I be able to afford to ship her back to Italy? The US government had been kind enough to have her brought here, but shipping a 3,000-pound piece of marble would cost much more than I could afford. But then again, what would I do without my Cleopatra? It was my destiny to have created her and I would miss her.

When the exposition was over, I made a heart-breaking choice: I put Cleopatra into storage.

I tried to make my departure less final. I fantasized to her and to myself that I would make so much money displaying my art that I could have her shipped back to Rome in no time. But I choked back tears after I turned to leave her.

The Statue

AFTER THE EXPOSITION ENDED, MY sculptor searched in vain for someone to buy me. No one in Philadelphia wanted me. Couldn't they see my grandeur? Didn't they recognize my noble spirit? Didn't they know it took millions of years to form me? The countless men who slaved to bring me to Rome and now here? The four painstaking years my sculptor had spent carving me?

It was even worse when tough characters came to encase me in my crate. They handled me carelessly, cursing my bulk. Their hammers pounded as they shut out the light. I was in a dark place again, like a ship's hold.

Edmonia Lewis

IN MY ROOMING HOUSE BED that night, I cried.

The next day I contacted some groups in California to see if they would exhibit my smaller pieces. The San Francisco Art Association said they would be happy to. Perhaps I could make enough money to have Cleopatra shipped back to Rome. I chose to show my work in California in the meager hope that if Samuel was still in California he would see the publicity about my exhibit and come to see me.

During those six long months that I had stood with Cleopatra at the Philadelphia Exposition, I wanted so much for a friend or family member to come and see her. I made a risky decision. Before I went to exhibit my work in San Francisco, I would seek out my family at Thunder Waters. If my Ojibwe family wouldn't come to me, I would go to them.

The next day I put on my customary artist garb; navy blue skirt, white blouse, ribbon tie, jacket, and red beret. I wished I still had some of my buckskins to wear, but I had slowly let them go. I settled the rent with my landlady and headed to the Philadelphia train station. When I reached Buffalo, I took one of the tourist carriages to Niagara.

It was a ten-mile ride to the Falls, but I didn't mind. I drank in the beauty of my beloved forests, and breathed in the smell of the tall pines.

It was autumn, and the trees created an ever-changing

display of red, yellow, and orange. To me, they represented life with all of its changes and surprises. A purple haze of campfire smoke hung over the trees and created a haze over the setting sun.

It was clear to me that some Great Spirit had made this land and wanted all to share its beauty. Just as I was thinking that, our carriage passed scarred places, where trees had once stood. Fenced-in houses further ruined the landscape.

The driver dropped me off. I had been such a city girl in Boston and Rome that it felt strange to pick my way down the tiny overgrown path that I hoped would lead to my family. Then I saw it: the wigwam. The birch bark shelter looked a little more ragged than it had in my youth, yet it was home.

Since night was falling, everyone was inside. At the flap, I announced, "Hello. It's me, Mary."

I heard whispering inside. I said, "I'm coming in."

I opened the flap, and the barrel of a rifle was my greeting.

A women's voice said in Ojibwe, "No, no, Father. It's Mary. Catherine's daughter."

Grumbling, my uncle put down the rifle. It took me a moment to catch my breath. Then, in the dim shadows lit only by a small campfire, I crouched down and in my best, almost forgotten Ojibwe, said, "I have missed all of you."

I was so glad to see Abequa. I hardly recognized her, but in the flickering light of the fire, I saw she had become a lovely, young woman with shiny black braids and a warm smile. She immediately came to me in our crouched wigwam walk and gave me a hug.

The rest of the family appeared none too thrilled. They looked at my white people's clothes and muttered words I could no longer understand. When I was young, the family had spoken in broken English. Now they only spoke Ojibwe. I wondered if we could still communicate.

Then Abequa spoke up, "The family is surprised by your clothing, although they shouldn't be. You've lived in the white world for so long."

"Where is Nokomis?"

"You remember how old she was, Mary. She died five winters ago."

"It seems strange not to see her stoking the fire."

When I looked around, I saw Uncle Ogima, Aunt Sarah, my younger male cousin, and Abequa. The group had dwindled since my mother and Nokomis died.

Everyone settled back to what they were doing, and I asked Abequa to walk with me to my rock. "It's getting dark, but I think we can find it," I said.

We walked arm in arm. Just that simple touch felt good.

When we arrived at my rock, we knelt to look at it. I saw my drawings and remembered what each one meant. The rock held records of the milestones of my life from the time my mother died until I left for Oberlin.

The next day I asked Abequa if she would help me find my mother's burial spot.

"I didn't get a chance to tell you; I'm working now, Mary."

"I'm not surprised. The way you wear your hair and care for your clothes. And your English—it's almost perfect!"

"I'm working at a souvenir shop on Goat Island. I

still can't read or write, but I can make change, and I like to talk with the customers. But I don't start work until the afternoon. So, let's find your mother's grave."

Before we left, I exchanged some simple Ojibwe phrases with my aunt and uncle. They barely looked up.

As Abequa and I searched through the forest, I asked her why my family was so cold to me.

"Remember how you felt, the way they treated you when you returned from McGraw? It's the same as now, except things are much worse."

She told me how the government was making everyone have a title for their land, a title they would have to pay for. She explained how her parents and their small band fought this rule. If they wouldn't cooperate, my cousin said, they would be forced to live on a reservation.

"Like where Grandma and Grandpa live?"

"Probably worse. On these new reservations, they will give us money to buy food, but no work. Nothing to do. My family can't bear to think about that."

We walked as we talked. Then Abequa said, "We're getting close. I remember that red bush." We had buried my Nimaamaa like Papa. Except, to honor my mother, my uncle had carved a bear - our band's totem - and placed it on the front of her spirit house.

We looked where we thought it would be. No luck, until I saw the wooden bear lying at a tilt nearly parallel to the ground. Leaves and vines covered the spirit house. We pulled them away.

"Nimaamaa!" I cried, and knelt down where she lay. I sprinkled the house with my tears.

209

Abequa put her arm around me. She spoke soothingly in Ojibwe.

Then I heard a familiar voice; "You have me, Mary. You will always have me."

I straightened up, turned to my cousin, and asked, "Did you hear someone speak?"

For once someone didn't look at me like I was demented. "Perhaps that was the spirit of your mother," Abequa said.

I felt shaky. I had thought that the voice–the gusts of wind, the cool sensations–were the ghost of Cleopatra. I was confused. All these years perhaps the voice was my mother's.

I had planned to stay with my family for two weeks, but with the icy attitude of my aunt and uncle, I decided to leave early. The day before I left, my uncle returned from the trading post with a letter addressed to my aunt in white man's language. I volunteered to read it. When I opened the letter, I saw it was Samuel's handwriting.

Dear Aunt and Uncle,

I wanted to let you know that I got married. I found a white woman. We are very happy. Her name is Melissa. She is a widow with six children.

I will send you more details once I get settled into a house with a real address.

Love,

Samuel

It felt like someone put an arrow through my heart. Why would he write to my aunt and uncle but not to me? Pride kept me from showing how hurt I felt.

While my relatives gibbered about the news, I excused myself and went outside. I ran to my rock, sat next to it, and cried. My aunt and uncle don't love me anymore, and now Samuel doesn't care! I didn't write on the rock. I didn't want anything to remind me of how Samuel had wounded me!

I promised myself, I will have to make it on my own, as usual. Art will save me. My exhibit in California will be a huge success. If Samuel happens to see an ad and come to an exhibition, fine. But, if not . . . These were brave words but they could not heal my heart.

I walked through the forest and called to the Great Spirit and my Catholic Jesus. Please stop this pain! I returned to the wigwam and acted as if nothing had happened.

That night I slept by Abequa. We talked, giggled, and lamented that neither of us had found someone to love... although I did tell her about Peter, and she had feelings for a French trader. She asked about Rome and I told her stories until we drifted off to sleep.

Next morning, I forced a smile and told everyone how much I loved them. I engaged in half hugs with Aunt Sarah and Uncle Ogima, and walked with Abequa to where I would get a carriage.

I told my dear cousin, "I will write and the priest can read my letters to you."

211

"Please do, Mary. I love to hear about your world. It's so exciting, compared to this place."

"You don't have it so bad here, Abequa. There is still much beauty at Thunder Waters."

We hugged, and I climbed into the carriage.

Transportation had improved since my trip to Boston so many years ago. To get from Buffalo to San Francisco only took a few transfers. It was November; cool enough to keep the windows closed. So, soot was not a problem.

The Pacific Appeal and The Elevator–both colored newspapers–ran advance stories about me before my arrival. I hoped that Samuel would notice.

My gallery opening brought out 150 white and colored citizens, reported the Pacific Appeal, whose papers reached coloreds up and down the coast. When asked who my influences were, I credited Harriet Hosmer and Hiram Powers. They were responsible for encouraging me at the beginning of my career. But I forgot to mention Mr. Brackett, who taught me a life lesson I couldn't forget.

At the exhibit, the colored community wanted to host a fancy reception for me, but, businesswoman that I was, I asked if they would save the cost of the reception to buy my bust of Abraham Lincoln. I had to sell all my statues before returning to Rome.

My marble pieces, Cupid Caught and The Wedding of Hiawatha, sold quickly. When my week-long exhibit ended, I moved my remaining pieces to the San Jose Market and later to the Catholic Fair. To counter competition from a free exhibition of paintings, I cut my admission price from 50 to 25 cents. I sold Awake -and Asleep to a wealthy San Francisco man.

As I mingled at these exhibitions, I kept looking for Samuel. Would he surprise me?

Several colored women marveled that I could make this long journey from Rome to California and back again, alone. Their admiration helped my confidence.

It took me a long time to get back to Rome. First across the continent and then across the Atlantic. Being alone on these travels gave me time to think. I had accomplished more than any other colored or Ojibwe woman. I had my successful run at the Centennial. I displayed and sold my art, while traveling from one side of the world to another.

But now what? I missed my Cleopatra more than family or friends. She had been my silent companion for most of my life, whether I had known it or not. Would I ever see her again, or feel her coolness? Aside from my love for her, she was my greatest accomplishment. With Cleopatra, I had risen beyond common classical art. I had done something new that caught the attention of the art world and the public: she wasn't just noble; she was human. And she wasn't European; she was Egyptian. But what good had it done? No one wanted to buy her statue. I wasn't sure I could continue to break new ground.

I received so much attention for being a colored, Indian sculptor, not all of it good. But it had kept my life exciting. Could I live without this? Had I reached the top? Would I sink into oblivion?

When I re-entered my workshop after months of

being away, I coughed. The windows and doors had been shut for so long that marble dust filled the air.

I threw open the doors and windows. The fresh air helped, but I couldn't stop thinking about Cleopatra, and how she was locked away in a dark place, so far from Rome.

The Statue

After my sculptor could find no buyer for me in Philadelphia, she shipped me by rail to another city. Jouncing around in the baggage car was the most uncomfortable journey of my life. The train sped north and west to a large inland sea with an Indian name, Michigan. The train stopped at the southern shore of this sea.

Not far from the shore stood an enormous building of brick and glass, topped by three domes: the Interstate Industrial Exposition Building. The door of my rail car slid open with a loud rasp and grey light flooded the car. The skies of this city were gray with smoke. They hoisted me onto another wagon, and sturdy horses hauled me to the building.

In front of the main entrance, an ornate fountain splashed. They carried me through wide doors into a huge gallery, filled with countless paintings and sculptures. Young Americans, like my sculptor, had produced these works. On display, there were even "Indian curiosities."

They positioned me in a place of prominence, and crowds of people came to study me. Some gazed at me for a long time but many hurried past. When children approached me, their mothers would grab their hands to lead them away.

Visitors didn't come just to see artwork. Other rooms displayed large modern machines. The organizers of the exhibit were showing the world that the city had risen from its ruins and would again become a great metropolis. When the exhibit closed, my creator again stored me in a dark place.

It was a large warehouse near a river. Men shoved me into a corner and forgot about me. These men wore rough work clothes. Their faces were smeared with dust mixed with sweat. They slaved in the warehouse for little pay. They spoke in a musical language. They joked bitterly about their tragic luck. They laughed at being stranded so far from home, in a land that didn't want them. They laughed so hard, they wiped their eyes from the merriment. They knew they had been hired only for their strong backs.

I sat there for 16 years, my sculptor thousands of miles away. She was scraping together the rent money to keep me safe. She even offered me to the new art museum, the one they built on the site of the exhibition building. The Art Institute would not take me. Was it due to my shocking lack of modesty or dark depiction of death?

In my final year in the warehouse, one of the workers showed he cared. Whenever the dust dulled my surface, he would lovingly wipe my surface with a wet rag. His name was Seamus Delaney. He wore woolen pants, heavy boots, and a tweed jacket, topped by a jaunty cap. He was short with a barrel chest. He had a handsome face accented by a deep cleft in his chin, like the cliffs of Ireland. His thick black hair had touches of gray.

Like my creator, he came from a tribal clan, who

prized family, story-telling, and making music. The two tribes shared another characteristic: their governments exploited and oppressed them.

This man fell in love with me. He would protect me and use me shrewdly. He was 49 years old, with a future of hard labor stretching ahead.

Seamus had worked hard on his Irish farm but it was nothing like this drudgery. He had grown up on a quarter-acre of land, not far from the sea. The soil was stony and barely supported their potatoes.

Their farm was on the banks of the Spiddal River, not far from the craggy west coast of Ireland. Their little patch had a stone hut with a thatched roof, and a small outhouse. A rock rubble wall surrounded it. Looking contentedly over this wall was the farm's one extravagance, a draught horse. The Delaneys had given him the mythic name, Bucephalus, in honor of Alexander's beloved steed.

PART TEN
OBLIVION

Edmonia Lewis
Thirty-Two to Thirty-Four Years Old
1876 - 1878

ARRIVING BACK IN ROME AFTER my trip to the States, I felt forlorn without my Cleopatra. Little did I know I would eventually see her again. I finally got myself moving by going to mass at St. Peter's.

The priests' chanting gave me comfort. Our aged pope–Pope Pius IX–insisted on saying one mass a day, although he had open sores on his legs. Sometimes, the priests had to carry him in.

Seeing the pope's courage, I took heart. I returned to my artwork. I heard that former President Ulysses S. Grant was making a world tour and would stop in Rome. I thought he might be staying at one of the fine hotels on Pincian Hill, which overlooked Rome. I decided to stake him out.

Within a few days, I saw a bustle of excitement and watchful guards. A handsome carriage pulled up and President and Mrs. Grant entered the hotel. Every day after that I brought my pad of paper and sketched him on the run. When I was done, I made a portrait of the president and waited to catch him leaving the hotel. I walked up to him, showed him the picture, and asked him if he would sit for final corrections.

"Why, that's remarkable, young lady!" he declared.

"Can you come to my studio tomorrow afternoon, so I can finish it?"

Of course, he wanted to see the portrait completed and didn't mind posing at my studio. When it was completed, he offered a large sum and I was pleased.

But even this success did not re-light my fires. I had to eat, though, so I took to the world of religious art. The pope himself helped me get commissions. Being one of a handful of colored people at St. Peter's masses, I stood out, and eventually the pope noticed me.

One day he asked the priests to bring me to his throne. "I am happy you come to mass so often. To whom do I have the pleasure?"

"I am Edmonia, Holy Father, Edmonia Lewis."

"I see." Then he asked the question I hated most, "Do you have family here?"

This opened a wound that would never heal. A tear slipped from my eye as I said, "No, not really. I guess you could say I'm married to my art."

This brought about a discussion of my work, and the pope said he knew of some churches and religious leaders who needed altarpieces. I thanked him and kissed his ring.

The commissions gave me enough money to live decently. I loved to visualize and sculpt religious figures, like our Lord Jesus and The Holy Mother.

But this kind of work was not satisfying. I liked being well known. I was used to being a controversial, young talent with an exotic background. Now, only in my 30s, I was becoming a "has been."

I thought about Cleopatra every day. She did not communicate with me. Perhaps she was angry that I had to crate her up and store her in a warehouse. In 1878---

two years after the Exposition---I heard that Chicago was holding what they called the Chicago Industrial Exposition to demonstrate how it had recovered from The Great Chicago Fire. A former county commissioner and admirer of my Cleopatra wrote to me and asked if I would like to show Cleopatra at the exhibition. The showing would not be as large and grand as the Philadelphia Centennial, but I could stay at his home with his wife and family. He tempted me by adding, "You may be able to sell Cleopatra in Chicago."

The cost and difficulty of the journey so soon after my last one did not please me. But the thought of seeing Cleopatra again and perhaps getting a buyer for her pulled me back to the States.

The way I acted when I saw Cleopatra was embarrassing. When four workmen let down the wooden sides of her crate, I rushed towards her and put my arms around her shoulders. The men looked surprised and walked away laughing. But oh, how I felt she still loved me when she sent her cool ripples.

Cleopatra was a big draw at the Expo, but it was a short run, and no one offered to purchase her. Someone from the Catholic House of the Good Shepherd asked if I would show Cleopatra at a weeklong exhibit at Farwell Hall to benefit the home. I did. Although people paid for admission and raved about how special she was, no one bought my queen.

I comforted myself with the knowledge that she probably enjoyed being on display again, but it tore me apart to put her back into storage. Awash in tears and worry, I said goodbye to Cleopatra once more.

When I returned to Rome, I was so disappointed about my statue that I took to my bed and hardly ate or drank. Why would no one buy her? Even when I inquired with the Art Institute in Chicago they didn't want her. Was it due to what Americans thought was her shocking lack of modesty. Was it because of my dark depiction of death? I lay in a state between sleep and wakefulness. I kept my Bible and bourbon close at hand, but neither helped.

Then one day I heard a knock. Although I knew I looked awful, I trudged to the door. When I opened it, I beheld the perfectly dressed Mrs. Massri. I tried to hide myself by folding my arms.

"Edmonia," she said with concern, "are you sick?"

"Not really. Well, maybe."

"What's wrong? I haven't seen you for some time."

I couldn't handle standing there looking so messy and her so perfect. So, I asked if I could come to see her the next day at the museum.

"Of course you can. But you must promise me that you will come . . . or I'll be back."

"All right, and thanks," I managed to say, closing the door in relief.

After she had given me the art history books a few years earlier, I had gone to see her and chat with her on many an afternoon. But I hadn't sought her out since the Philadelphia Centennial Exhibition.

When I went to the museum the next day, I laid everything out—the joys and sorrows of people's reactions at the Centennial, not finding a good home for Cleopatra, and my uncertainty about where my career was headed.

When I finished, Mrs. Massri said, "You have accomplished so much, Edmonia, creating such an innovative piece of work. Having the statue displayed at the Centennial Exposition and then in Chicago; it's all quite fantastic! I am not sure why no one has bought it. Perhaps it's too sad for someone's home. But a museum should want it. You know there aren't many art museums yet, but more will come."

I was quiet, thinking of The Art Institute's rejection.

"I understand your uncertainty about what to do next. You have a right to be worried. I study the latest trends in the art world." She sighed and looked at me sympathetically. "The revival of classical art, sad to say, is going out of style."

I shook my head as if to dismiss this possibility.

"The center of great art is no longer Rome. It's Paris."

"Really? I've been so busy working and traveling that...."

Mrs. Massri gave me a suggestion. "You should go to Paris. A group of painters known as "Impressionists" has created a movement, and a young man named Rodin is changing the world of sculpture. Perhaps you could visit his workshop and get some ideas."

I smiled and said, "I just might do that."

For the next few weeks, I kept myself busy working on a church altarpiece, but at night I twisted and turned.

A bit of happiness came my way, though, when I received a letter from Samuel. He told me how he had settled with his wife and her children in Bozeman, Montana. I felt like singing.

I took the train to Paris. I would look at paintings by the new "Impressionists," and visit Rodin's studio.

On my train trip, I experienced more fear than I had on any of my other journeys. The climb up the mountains was steep, and the sharp turns we made—I couldn't look. When the train reached the highest peaks, older passengers gasped for air. One woman screamed.

Then all of a sudden I heard and felt a long, drawn out gust of wind. My hair flared out, but no one else's did.

Startled as usual, I said, "Is that you, Cleopatra?"

The properly dressed woman next to me, said, "What?"

"I'm sorry. I was just talking to myself."

After that wind from nowhere, I felt calm and safe even though we continued to go up and down steep mountains. Was this Cleopatra or some other spirit helping me? I didn't question any further…I was just relieved to feel so relaxed.

The streets of Paris dazzled me. I loved the architecture of the churches, especially Notre Dame and Sacre Coeur. Many buildings had tall, thin spires that reached to the heavens. The Seine River with its sculpted stone bridges enticed me to take a tour boat, just for the fun of it.

I enjoyed eating at the outdoor bakeries and browsing

through the city bookstores. Finally, I got serious about why I came to Paris. I asked where Rodin's studio was and found my way there.

I walked into the open door of the workshop. There was a buzz of activity. Several young men were busy working with bronze.

In the middle of it all, a young man was sitting, creating a clay model. Behind him were two bronze sculptures of modern-looking people doing everyday things. Their every tendon and muscle stood out, and the figures looked very intense. They were like my idealized sculptures of heroic people; however, their features were out of proportion— some had very large hands or feet.

"Can I help you?' asked the young artist. He was dressed in a dirty white shirt and suspenders and appeared to be about my age. He looked as intense as his figures.

"I have heard great things about you and was just curious." I said as I smiled.

Rodin pulled at his long bushy beard and said, "I am just doing what I have to do."

I politely mentioned how his sculptures had larger than normal features. He smiled. "I'm glad you noticed. Usually it is to emphasize something. Like over here." He pointed to a clay figure. "I'm trying to depict a man lost in thought. His hands are much larger than usual."

"How about those men over there, with the ropes around their necks?"

"Those are the Burghers of Calais. In the 1300s the English were going to hang them, and this shows them going to what they thought was their death."

"Thought?"

"At the last minute, they were given a reprieve and were not executed."

"I see how you have made their arms unusually long… as if they're folding under a great weight."

"You are quite right. I also gave each man a different expression, as he fears what's ahead."

"Very interesting," I said. "Well, I am an art lover like you. I will leave you to your work. I really do admire it."

After thanking me, his attention quickly returned to his clay model.

At the door, I looked back. "Do you ever work in marble?"

He looked up. "Marble is a thing of the past. Bronze is the future."

I headed to a bistro and ordered a cup of coffee. Coffee pots clanked, people talked and smoked, but I was deep in thought. So, this was the new wave—to portray common activities and distort people's bodies for emphasis. In bronze. I didn't think I could do that. I preferred to sculpt people as realistically as possible… sometimes showing emotion… with perfect proportions. I liked working with marble. Bronze seemed so cold.

⌇⌇⌇

Upon returning to Rome, I went to Mrs. Massri's office. She was glad to see me.

"I did it. I went to Paris. I even spoke with Rodin."

She leaned forward. "What was he like?"

226

"Intense. He told me that my kind of art is out of style."

"Oh, I was afraid so," she said, with sad eyes.

"I don't want to work in bronze, or to create his kind of art."

We sat quietly together for a while, like Rodin's sculpted man who was deep in thought.

Eventually I said, "I have to escape Rome where there are so many expectations of me. I don't want to return to America. Too much judgment there."

"Is it really necessary to leave Rome?"

"Yes."

My mentor crooked her head to one side and frowned.

The Statue

AS SEAMUS DID HIS MINDLESS work in the warehouse, his thoughts returned to Bucephalus. Seamus' family used him to plow the field, fertilize their crops, and bring their meager harvest to market. Bucephalus was always in a good mood, even when he was working. He was calm around little children but could be tough when needed.

The year Seamus was born, a disease had spread to Ireland. It devastated the island's potato crop, starving its people. When Seamus was 18, the sheriff and landlord came to evict the Delaneys. The sheriff also led Bucephalus away, a sight Seamus would never forget.

Seamus admired me in the half-darkness of the warehouse, but was certain we would soon have to part. My sculptor finally had failed to keep up her payments. His boss told him they would throw me out at the end of the week.

Seamus had orders to move me outside to a pile of waste. He could not see discarding such a prize, especially because he had a better use for me. He knew a man in the city who would pay any price for such a treasure. He owed this man money and I could settle his debt.

After leaving the warehouse one day, Seamus sauntered into a lively bar on South Clark Street called the Mitre. It was an upscale establishment, with a tin ceiling and an expansive mirror behind the bar. He would normally not frequent such a place. But Seamus had a burning purpose to spend a little extra pay at the Mitre. Its owner was the man he owed money. Blind John Condon was the leading gambler in the city. He controlled racetracks in Chicago and across the U.S. As Seamus paid a full dime for his stein, he casually asked the bartender if Johnny was in.

The bartender pointed upstairs to Condon's office. "I hope you're holding what Johnny wants, or he'll be yelling at me for letting you up."

Seamus climbed the stairs and stepped into Condon's well-furnished office. Blind John was standing, facing a tall window, puffing on a thick cigar, and gazing down on the commotion on Clark Street.

He was a tall man with shrewd eyes that were gradually failing him. He wore a brush moustache that had grown gray. He had heavy jowls and a double chin. He was immaculately dressed in a natty suit. Even indoors, he sported his bowler hat.

Condon turned toward Seamus with a stern look. It was difficult to tell where his weak eyes were focused. "So, how ya' makin' out at your job?" Condon inquired, without much interest. He flicked some ash.

"I make enough to eat and the occasional drop," Seamus confessed, "but not enough to pay you what I owe."

"Oh," Condon said, good-naturedly, "Well, it's much more now. You know, lad, you shouldn't wager what you don't have."

"I was just trying to get ahead, Johnny. I thought your filly couldn't lose on that muddy track."

"Well, if you don't have my money, why'd you come?"

"Johnny, I know how you love beautiful things. The warehouse has something you want. It's worth twice what I owe. You've got to see her."

Condon was intrigued. He called for his buggy. They soon pulled into the yard behind the warehouse. I was there but all Condon could see at first was a white ghost. He walked carefully to where I was seated, stepping around other objects headed to the scrap heap.

"Oh, she's a big one," he exclaimed to Seamus. Condon was an avid collector of art and I was one piece he couldn't resist.

The man with the failing eyes stroked my features in the warehouse yard. He fingered every crevice and fold. As he did so, his face dissolved into a broad smile. "Don't tell me Seamus, is it her?"

"Yes, Johnny, we know who she is and she's worth at least a thousand. I'll let you haul her away for free."

Condon continued to stroke my skin. "She's not yours to give, but I'll gladly take her. We'll forget that little unpleasantness, but don't let me catch you coming to my track. It's for sports, not little men like you."

Bewitched by my beauty, Condon immediately moved me to the Mitre, where I became the center of attention. Men gawked at me amid the bustle. They thought I was their bawdy woman, posing for them in my naked splendor. They ignored my tragic pose.

After lonely years in the warehouse, I enjoyed the liveliness of the place. The piano badly needed tuning but made merry music for the patrons. They were almost all men. They drank, spat, and smoked, before staggering home. Condon was often there, playing for high stakes. He was pleased that I was drawing a higher class crowd. The connoisseurs from the fine art galleries dropped around to see me. They called it slumming.

When he wasn't minding the saloon, Condon presided over his Harlem Race Track, directly west of the city. Thoroughbreds pounded around the dusty oval in front of a large grandstand. Blind John made sure he was sitting there in his box when his young filly, Cleopatra, ran.

One day, Seamus splurged again at the Mitre, just to visit me. Condon noticed him standing before me, completely entranced. He called him over to his table.

"Doesn't she brighten the place?" the gambler exclaimed, glancing toward me. "I don't think I've thanked you properly." Condon looked at Seamus thoughtfully. "How would you like to work for me?"

Seamus was surprised by the offer. "I tried work as a bouncer in New York. I was still too weak from the hunger to throw anyone out. So, they had me wash dishes. No thanks."

"Not here, man, but at my track. Didn't you tell me once you loved horses?"

"What's the pay?"

"Ah, why is it always about money? You'll be outdoors. You'll be tending the finest thoroughbreds."

"You still have that filly, don't you?" Seamus interrupted. "The one who cost me my shirt."

Condon's dim eyes filled with a faint gleam. "She's my treasure and someday she'll earn her keep. Tell you what, if you're a good man around horses, I'll pay a dollar over what that warehouse pays." They shook on it.

The next day, Seamus took pleasure in telling off his boss and marching out of the gloom into the sunlight. He took the streetcar to the Harlem Race Track. It stopped right in front for the convenience of the degenerates and swells who swarmed there. Seamus reported to the office bearing a brief hand-written note from Condon.

A trainer led Seamus to the backstretch and handed him a pitchfork. Seamus spent his days mucking out foul-smelling stalls. His favorite stall, of course, belonged to that feisty filly, Cleopatra. At three years old, she was just coming into her prime. They kept her on a strict diet but he snuck her apples.

Cleopatra was 16 hands high and considered plump by her handlers. Except for a splash of white on her nose, she was coal black, clear to her tail. She had slender legs with long taut muscles that needed much massaging. Though Seamus was approaching 50, he was nothing but an overgrown stable boy, and the trainers didn't allow him to touch her.

As spring passed into summer, Seamus showed the trainers that he was quick to learn and indeed had a way with horses. They promoted him to hot walker. There was nothing more delightful than leading Cleopatra around the track on a frosty morning.

Finally, the trainers instructed Seamus on how to wrap a thoroughbred's ankles. This was more of an art than a science. He had to have the right touch to make them just right.

On the Fourth of July, the grandstand bore bunting and the crowd was close to bursting. They had come to see the races and would stay for fireworks. The genteel throng sat in the boxes, the working-class families filled the infield. The carefully groomed track was a mile long and 80 feet wide.

Back in the stables, Seamus was readying Cleopatra for her eleventh race. She seemed more spirited than usual. After he had her saddled up, he proudly led her to the track. Cleopatra and her jockey were clothed in my ceremonial colors; draped in the deepest purple. The crowd applauded at the first sight of her. Blind John prayed this would be the race where she would repay him.

When the race began, the black filly surged to third, responding to the furious whip of her jockey. Seamus' heart swelled as she chased the leader down the backstretch. She galloped into the lead, first by a nose, then by a length. The fans were cheering her on hysterically, especially the women. Seamus was right by the rail when he heard the sound he would never forget.

It was startling, like the report of a pistol, as two bones in her right leg snapped. This didn't stop Cleopatra. She stumbled forward, as her jockey frantically reigned her back. Then she mercifully came to a stop, her right hoof dangling. Cleopatra made no complaint. She did not whinny in her agony. The track was deep in silence. Seamus could hear little girls and their mothers weeping.

Seamus and the other handlers rushed to her side. Sobbing, Seamus stroked her back and buried his face in her tossing neck. "There, there," he murmured, his face blinded by tears, "you'll be alright, girl. "Getting her off the track gave Seamus and the others all they could handle. The filly refused to believe her race was over. As they walked her back to her stall, Blind John Condon fell in beside Seamus. His weak eyes were wet.

Back in the stables, they worked to fit her right leg with a cast. Cleopatra balked. How could she race with such a contraption? She spun bizarrely on the floor, as if she was still racing. She shook the cast off. Blind John and Seamus stared at each other in despair. Condon gave a nod to the vet and left the stall. They were walking away when Seamus heard another unforgettable sound. Cleopatra now belonged to the ages.

Blind John hastily arranged a funeral to honor her. He had her buried outside the backstretch. Her nose, splashed with white, pointed toward the finish line.

After the burial, Condon regained his composure. He telegraphed the Mitre and instructed that they transport me to the track immediately. I was once again rolling through the streets of Chicago toward an uncertain destination.

When we reached the Harlem Race Track, they carefully positioned me in front of a mound of fresh earth. This would be my home for the next 70 years. I would be buffeted by wind and rain, assaulted by snow and sleet. The mound of earth would subside over the years and fill with water, and a small pond would reflect my beauty.

Ten years after they placed me to watch over Cleopatra's grave, the horses stopped running at the Harlem Race Track. Racecars now roared down the backstretch, spewing smoke and fumes. Seamus knew nothing about fixing these machines. He lost his job but had a better fate than his boss.

In 1915, Blind John Condon became something of a statue like me. Paralysis struck him and he never recovered. The king of high rollers, who made a million dollars during one summer of racing at Harlem Race Track, the man who honored the memory of his prized filly with my majesty, died on August 10, 1915.

PART ELEVEN
RESTORATION AND REBIRTH

Edmonia Lewis
Thirty-Five to Sixty-Three Years Old
1879 - 1907

For once, I didn't make any quick decisions. I continued doing marble altarpieces. The money was good. Mr. Story kept up his workshop down the street from mine. One day I bumped into him at a cafe. He wasn't wearing his usual pompous look.

"How's business?" he asked. "Are people still flocking to see the colored prodigy?"

"My business is probably about the same as yours."

He harrumphed and walked away.

Eventually, I took a large room in a building near the top of one of Rome's hills. I had a commanding view of the city, and I took pleasure in my new place. There was enough room for me to do small marble pieces for churches. It was also a great place to hide.

But then something happened that set me on edge. The great abolitionist Frederick Douglass and his wife sought me out when they were touring Europe. Their son had served in the Negro regiment headed by Colonel Shaw. They had purchased a bust of the fallen hero.

Mr. Douglass had gained weight and his hair had grayed, but he still wore it long and untamed. His jaw was set in its familiar position and his eyes could still burn a hole through you. The Douglasses were impressed with where I lived. We talked about how it was not easy for coloreds in the States, even though they were now citizens.

I became quiet, though, when Mrs. Douglass said, "We haven't heard anything about your work back in America." She paused for a moment and asked, "What happened?"

She may not have meant anything by her question, but it worried me. The next day I just about ran to Mrs. Massri's office. For the first time, I found her door closed. There were no other offices in the corridor. I looked around for someone on the Vatican staff. I ran down to the tapestry hall where Jesus' eyes followed me.

Where could she be?

I finally saw someone wearing a museum uniform. Noticing that I was in a state, the man led me to the main office.

A middle-aged woman with spectacles on the tip of her nose told me, "Mrs. Massri was called back suddenly to Egypt due to an illness in her family. We don't know when or if she will be back."

I was stunned. "Did she leave any message for me, Edmonia Lewis?"

"No, it was sudden. No messages."

I walked ever so slowly back to my place on the hill.

I would have to solve my problems on my own. Mrs. Douglass' question confirmed my fears that I, Edmonia Lewis, the Indian, colored child prodigy, was now a "has been." I could not accept that.

I started packing. I had to leave my marble behind. I settled with my landlord.

Where would I go?

It had to be an English-speaking place. I didn't want to learn a new language. And it must be far from Rome. By the time I had finished packing, I had decided to go to London. I would leave word for no one. I would let them remember my triumphs. My absence would be a great mystery, and I would keep my legacy and reputation. Maybe it wouldn't be so bad sinking into oblivion.

I stuffed all of my worldly goods into two carpetbags. I boarded a steamship. The journey was smooth. When I got to London, rain and fog greeted me. I had no idea where I would stay. I went to a local bookstore, bought a map of London, and sat down at a shop that served tea. I had just arrived but already I missed Rome's sunshine and my strong Italian coffee.

Sipping from a fancy cup, I suddenly remembered that my wealthy client, the Marquess of Bute, had told me about an estate in the Hammersmith district of London. He had mentioned that he loved living in Hammersmith, because it had a Catholic church, a convent for teaching sisters, an almshouse, and an orphanage for girls. I would fit in well with these outsiders.

To get to Hammersmith, I had to take a boat up the Thames. When I got off at the dock, the rain came down harder. I was on a main street lined with houses and shops. Further in the distance, I saw the spire of a church and several buildings adjoining it. This had to be the place the marquess had mentioned.

Clumping through the rain, I looked for an inn. When I finally entered the door of a hotel, I was soaked through and shivering. I rented a room for the night and cleaned myself up, before looking for a place the next day. Eventually, I saw a three-story Victorian brick house at 154 Blythe Road that had a small wooden sign hanging from its porch, "Room for Rent."

The Statue

BLIND JOHN CONDON HAD TAKEN care of me in recent years. Four months after he died, a girl was born in Forest Park. She would grow to cherish me and protect me. Her parents christened her Loretta Licht. Like most residents of the town, her parents had emigrated from Germany. They heard German spoken from the pulpits of Forest Park's Lutheran churches and read the local newspaper in their native language. Loretta's father, Henry, was the greenskeeper for the Harlem Golf Course, which began life on the infield of the old racetrack.

Blind John had launched this enterprise in 1910 and his son, Jack, took over the operation following his father's death. Jack was cut from the same colorful cloth as his father. He had an adventurous spirit and traveled extensively.

After Jack married his fiancé, Marguerite, the couple spent their honeymoon in Europe and the Middle East. They brought back flowers from the Holy Land and gave them to the greens keeper's daughter.

After his father built the first nine holes, Jack added nine more, to make it the first 18-hole layout in the area, open to the public. Jack was determined to make the golf course a success.

When he finished building the course, I was smack in the middle of the 14th fairway. My little pond became the first of many water hazards.

To protect his property, Jack imported a German Shepherd. Like many of the townspeople, Otto spoke German. He patrolled the fairways morning to sundown. When he caught someone sneaking on, he would grip them by the sleeve.

The dog wasn't the only pet on the premises. A tame raccoon, nicknamed Bogey, would perch on the greenskeeper's shoulder. Loretta adored her father and thought he had the best job in the world.

My bulk, however, was an obstacle to his mower, as well as a torment to the golfers. They thought it unfair that I penalized them for shots right down the heart of the fairway. Jack was adamant, though, that I could not be disturbed from my vigil over his father's fallen filly.

He continued to create what he called, "A country club for the masses." He constructed a three-story clubhouse. It had a revolutionary feature: a women's locker room. It was one of the few courses to allow female golfers. It even offered them lessons.

Jack hired the finest teaching pro and paid William Philpot's passage from Edinburgh to take up residence above the caddy shack.

From an early age, Loretta and her brother sat at the caddy shack, waiting for golfers to hire them. Loretta carried their clubs and told them which ones to use. Besides the money she earned, she got free lessons from the Scotsman.

Like my creator, Loretta was dedicated to her craft and preferred to pursue it in solitude. She played alone so she wouldn't have men correcting her swing. It also helped her concentrate. It was especially tough for her to concentrate when I was in the way. Of all the wonders of the golf course, I was Loretta's favorite, though I cost her strokes. She also worried the white balls striking me might damage my flesh.

Loretta asked her father to provide me with some protection. He planted thick shrubs behind me, to shield me from the white missiles.

Living on the course amidst the foliage and wildlife, Loretta and her family felt far away from the urban commotion that surrounded them. The Harlem Golf Course was their sanctuary.

When Loretta was a teenager, a certain person invaded this sanctuary. Loretta was playing alone at dusk when she heard Otto barking. Loretta headed toward the commotion. Otto had sunk his teeth into the sleeve of an intruder. The young man was petrified. His face was white as he tried to yank his arm away from the dog. Otto would not let go until Loretta commanded him to "Aus!"

The young man was relieved to have his arm freed. "What are you doing here?" Loretta demanded. The fury shone in her eyes. He removed his cap.

"I'm sorry, Miss, I was just trying to get some shots in before dark."

"Oh," she said with heavy sarcasm, "It's customary to pay for that privilege at the pro shop."

"I know, Miss, but I can't afford to pay the full fee." He gazed at her sheepishly, hoping for forgiveness.

She peered at him in the gathering darkness. "What's your name?"

"Carl," he stammered, "Carl Woeltje. Don't you recognize me? I go to St. Paul Lutheran, same as you."

Loretta told the young man to come with her. "My father has a way to deal with trespassers like you." They walked toward the shimmering lights of the clubhouse, Otto trotting behind. Loretta found her father in his office, his face buried in a mountain of bills. He wore a worried expression; he was unsure how long Jack Condon could support this enterprise and keep him on salary.

"Ah, Loretta, it was even too dark for you. Don't tell me you finally found a partner."

She sighed, "No, Otto caught this one sneaking onto the second hole. His name is Carl. He goes to St. Paul's. I guess he's a church-going thief."

Henry looked sternly at Carl. "This course is losing enough money, without characters like you. Fortunately, we have a way for you to pay your fee." He led Carl to the kitchen, where the dishes from the evening meal were stacked. "This will pay for your round. Loretta, show him what to do."

Carl washed, while Loretta dried. When they were finished, she asked to see his swing.

Carl looked startled, "You mean, right here?" Loretta nodded.

Carl unfurled a herky-jerky swing, striking the kitchen floor much too roughly. Loretta giggled. "Who taught you that swing?"

"I can't afford lessons," Carl confessed. "I'm just trying to learn on my own."

"I can give you a lesson," Loretta offered. Carl suggested they play on Sunday, after church. Loretta agreed, but said she could not sit with him in the pew, because people would think they were dating.

Every Sunday, when the weather was fair, Loretta and Carl fled the church and headed to her sanctuary.

One afternoon, Carl struck a perfect shot that disappeared in the shrubs protecting my throne. He slammed down his club in disgust. Loretta berated him. "Look what you did!" pointing down at the gouge in her father's fairway. "When are you going to grow up?" she demanded. "You've got to control your temper, or you'll never be any good."

Carl felt as sheepish as the day he got caught sneaking in. "I'll work on it, but this statue–it doesn't belong here." He poked through the bush looking for his ball. Loretta remained miffed.

"She was here before you were born and she'll be here after you're dead. Forget your stupid ball and just look at her."

I must admit I looked magnificent that day, under blue skies, my reflection captured by my pond. Carl and Loretta paused to admire me. Then his gaze shifted to her. "Isn't there something we can do, besides golf? I've finished my apprenticeship at the print shop. I have a few bucks now. We could go to the Lido, or out for ice cream."

"I'm not allowed to see movies on Sunday," she countered, "and we can have ice cream in the clubhouse."

Carl set down his bag and clumsily grabbed her hand. "Loretta, I like you. Can't we be alone sometime?"

"We're alone right now," she said stubbornly, "And it's your shot." Carl sighed and dropped a new ball beside my pond. Loretta kept her stern expression, but, inside, her heart was melting. After he struck his ball onto the 14th green, he started to walk. Loretta stopped him. "First, tell her you're sorry." Carl laughed. He turned and patted me. He whispered, "I don't know who's more difficult, you or her."

During its storied history, the magnificent clubhouse would host but a single wedding. A young printer married a greenskeeper's daughter. In the cool evening, Loretta's laughter could be heard tinkling down from the veranda. The young bride didn't know it would be her last happy moment at the Harlem Golf Course.

Jack Condon's spendthrift ways had finally drained his bank account. He had to sell the golf course. The best offer came from an industrialist who proposed building a manufacturing plant on the site. Jack reluctantly agreed to the deal.

Loretta was devastated. So was her father. To lose his livelihood and his carefully landscaped course seemed unthinkable. However, when construction began, the reality was far worse than he and his family could imagine.

Before construction began, Loretta went to the clubhouse to collect her belongings. Among them was her scrapbook, where she had pressed the star-like petals the Condons had brought her from Bethlehem.

A portly official pulled up to the clubhouse. "U. S.

Naval Ordnance Plant. Official Car, Amertorp Corp." was stenciled on his car. He wore a dark suit and a perpetual scowl. Two trim naval officers were waiting for him.

It was 1938 and war was clearly coming. Companies with foresight were shifting from home goods to turning out weapons. American Can Company proposed building a plant to manufacture torpedoes on the site of the golf course. The Navy agreed to oversee the operation and purchase the underwater missiles.

The official and the officers sat in the defunct dining room. A stocky, unimposing man joined them. He removed his hat to reveal thinning gray hair. He was 69 years old but had the vitality of a much younger man. He put in long days at his office and traveled the country from one commission to the next.

His name was Albert Kahn, and he was an artist like my sculptor. Kahn had risen to become the leading industrial architect in America. His father was a rabbi and his mother an artist. When he was 11, Albert and his family left their native Prussia and arrived in Detroit. He later came to be known as "the man who built Detroit," constructing over 400 buildings in that city.

After earning his degree in architecture, Albert got a job in the fledgling auto industry. He designed Henry Ford's first modern plant and later his colossal River Rouge factory. The rabid anti-Semite and the son of a rabbi formed an unlikely team.

Like my creator, Albert liked the neoclassical style, echoing the grandeur of Rome and Athens. He designed neo-classic buildings for the University of Michigan campus. Now, as World War II approached, he was busy designing buildings to manufacture weapons on an unthinkable scale.

The plant official and naval officers pored over his blueprints. After they approved these plans, work began on the site.

Though it horrified her, Loretta was so fascinated by the project that she visited the site every chance she got. The workers carved a road through the club's stately entrance. Then, armies of men attacked the trees with saws. Loretta almost cried when they took down her favorite maple. She later told a reporter, "It was the most perfect tree and it was taken down for the war. The war changed everything."

Bulldozers destroyed the delicate greens and gouged the pristine fairways. It was destruction on an incredible scale. Loretta literally couldn't believe her eyes, as her favorite spot in the entire world was transformed into a sea of mud.

I was the only bright spot on the landscape. My beauty so impressed Albert Kahn that he insisted I stay where I was. The workers surrounded me with a temporary fence and took care to avoid me with their huge machines. They weren't so respectful of my little pond, which disappeared into the muddy mess.

For four years, the noise and work continued. When the plant was finished, a statue and a single, lonely spruce remained, the only survivors of the Harlem Golf Course.

Edmonia Lewis

IT WASN'T EASY LIVING IN a single room and not having my

sculpture pieces, especially my Cleopatra. By my second night on Blythe Road, loneliness had just about swallowed me.

Then the voice came softly and sweetly, "You have me. You will always have me."

I asked, "Is that you Cleopatra? Please say more. It's so nice to hear from you." But I remembered how I had heard those same words when I went to my mother's graveside. So, I blurted out, "Could it be you, Nimaamaa?"

It was a comfort to hear that mysterious voice return and say, "You have me, Mary. You will always have me." On the next day, my old determination returned. I awoke with my mind full of errands.

I planned to find the local bank, shoemaker, and various other shops that would meet my needs. By mid-morning, the mouth-watering aroma of freshly baked bread enticed me toward a bakery.

When I stepped inside, a tall, burly man with a handlebar moustache boomed, "Guten Morgen, Frau!"

I nodded and admired shelves of freshly baked breads and pastries. Then the voice of a young woman brought my eyes up to hers. "Do you see anything you like?"

I found myself smiling for the first time in London. "It all smells so good."

Like the man, she was dressed in all baker's white. The young woman was about two feet taller than I was. She had flowing blonde hair, and soft blue eyes the color of robin's eggs. Her looks were the exact opposite of mine, although I now took pride in my tawny brown skin and velvety brown eyes. I bought a loaf of rye and began a friendship with this young woman named Gretchen.

I invited Gretchen to come to my room for tea on Tuesday afternoons. We discussed every topic; about how she had had to learn English and felt out of place in London, why her family left Germany. One day, she asked me to help her knead the dough. It felt so good to use my hands again, to ply a substance so close to clay. Whenever she needed me, I helped with the kneading. It made me feel useful again.

I told Gretchen about my life. I started with my birth in Greenbush, and described my accomplishments in the art world–how I now wanted to enjoy a quiet life. At this early stage of getting to know each other, I left out the pain still etched my heart from the loss of my parents, and being almost beaten to death at Oberlin.

As the years rolled by, I enjoyed the simple pleasures of life: a walk in the countryside, a good English meat pie, a hearty ale. But the English tea would never substitute for my Italian coffee.

One day, I decided to write a letter to Samuel in Montana:

Dear Samuel,

Wouldn't Papa be surprised to know what we have accomplished? You are a highly respected barber and businessmen in Montana where only a few colored families live. And I have created sculptures that were all the talk in the art world for two decades. He would be so proud.

Your loving sister,

Edmonia

I quickly received a reply.

Dear Edmonia,

How do you know that Papa is not aware of what we have done? Remember his Lwa, and his cross with chains that symbolized the crossroads in life. Do you recall how Mother said, "Sometimes the things that are not seen are as important as the ones that are"?

Just think about it, my dear Sister.

Love,

Samuel

Before I could give his words much thought, I felt a sharp pain. Something on my right side under my ribs hurt. I had trouble breathing. When my landlady knocked on my door and announced that my usual Tuesday visitor, Gretchen, was there, I hardly stirred. "Tell her I'm sick and I'll see her another time."

Gretchen came up, anyway. "I won't be sent away that easily."

The Statue

AFTER FOUR YEARS OF CONSTRUCTION, the torpedo plant was finished. Albert Kahn, the man whose vision turned America into the Arsenal of Democracy, died on December 8, 1942, shortly after the commander cut the ribbon for the new plant. The munitions giant would turn out 9,000 torpedoes during the war. Navy pilots dropped some of them into the waters of Manila Bay and praised their performance.

During the war, the government built houses for the naval officers who oversaw the plant's construction and operation. Seven brick houses sat in a horseshoe around an expanse of green. I was in a position fitting my stature, right in the center. The children of the naval officers played with me. The younger ones took comfort sitting in my lap. I was their sanctuary during games of tag.

I was still in good shape. My complexion looked weathered, but my features were still intact. I was a curiosity to the many young children who lived in the horseshoe.

The commander, though, considered me a disgrace, completely out of place at a naval facility. He ordered his men to build a wooden enclosure to hide me from the world, especially from the children.

One enterprising boy loosened one of the boards and charged a quarter for a peek at the "naked lady." People were paying to see me for the first time in years! Then a new commander arrived and ordered the enclosure be removed. This exposed my beauty to the world but also to danger.

The attack came on Halloween night, 1971. Some teenage boys had bought cans of green and blue spray paint. Before they went on their destructive spree, they stoked their courage by sharing a six-pack of malt liquor in the cemetery. As the drink took effect, one of them proposed toppling a nearby tombstone. They easily pushed it off its pedestal.

This was such great fun, they knocked over three more, before tiring of the game. Then they spotted me on the other side of the fence. It would be a challenge to push over the naked lady. They climbed the fence into naval housing. They gathered in front of me and rattled their cans of paint. They scrawled crude words across my face and breasts. Pleased with their graffiti, they tossed down their cans and started to push.

I would not budge. The boys tried to rock me but I was simply too heavy. They became frustrated. One of them pounded on me with his sweaty fist. He proposed the idea for their final attack. They searched in the darkness for rocks and found some of suitable size. My whiteness made me an easy target, and they hurled their stones at my body.

They were Vandals, like the ones who sacked Rome. I stood helpless as a well-aimed rock crashed into my face. It broke off my nose. Another struck my chin, digging a deep gouge. They pelted my breasts and took special satisfaction from hitting my exposed one. The onslaught continued, until a light snapped on inside one of the houses. The boys grabbed their cans of spray paint and fled into the darkness. The next morning, the residents were dismayed to see my nose missing, my chin disfigured, and my breasts destroyed.

At that time, though, they had bigger concerns than me. The defense department was shutting down the torpedo plant. It had produced countless rockets and artillery fuses for the Korean and Vietnam War. Now, it was going to be a shopping mall.

Edmonia Lewis

"Maybe you need a doctor," Gretchen said, when she saw the pain in my eyes.

"You know what? I'm feeling better already. I'll sit at the table and we can talk. I don't want any tea."

"Sure, Miss Lewis." Gretchen used my last name, a sure sign I was aging.

"Lying here for the last few days, I have done some thinking. I was thinking that my greatest strengths were my greatest weaknesses."

"How so?"

"I tried to make friends at school when I was young by turning everything into a joke. It kept me from sitting in my room alone. But it got me into trouble, especially this one time."

Before she could ask what happened, I continued, "My other strength—I wanted to be the best at whatever I did."

Gretchen looked puzzled. "Was that so bad?"

"Working hard, alone, I never found someone to love, although . . ." I paused, thinking of Peter. "There was a young man. We knew each other for only a short while. But, it was a kind of love."

"You never told me!"

"I didn't know him for long" Then I changed the subject. "I accomplished great things through pure determination, but it sometimes caused jealousy in others, especially other artists. I could have been friends with a circle of woman artists in Rome but I was too competitive."

I paused for a while. "I never felt like I belonged anywhere."

"I feel for you, Edmonia."

It had taken me thirty years to get Gretchen to call me Edmonia instead of "Miss Lewis." She always wanted to show me so much respect, but being called "Miss Lewis" made me feel like an old spinster. Speaking of spinsters, Gretchen was now about forty-five years old and had never married. I saw the crow's feet forming around her eyes, but in comparison to me she was a youngster. She had been such a good friend over the years.

I continued, "From the age of twelve on, I was mostly with white people. The way the whites looked at me . . . but perhaps I made too much of it."

Gretchen touched my hand. "Your brown skin and your curly hair are very pretty. Actually, I like being with people who are different from me, as long as they don't make fun of my accent."

We both laughed a little.

"You're a special person, Gretchen."

I thought for a while and said, "But, again, my weakness was my strength. Being so aware of racial cruelty in the United States is what caused me to create my greatest statues: freed slaves and my Ojibwe people. These statues helped thousands look at my people with new respect."

"I would love to see those sculptures."

"That's kind of you. It's only now—at this very moment—that I understand something." I paused, trying to find the right words. "My happiest moments were when I was creating. Coming up with ideas, gouging out marble, refining it, polishing it."

I was having a little trouble with my breathing, but I had to voice my new insights. "When I look back now, loved ones come and go. Sometimes they bring happiness, sometimes disappointment. The joy you can depend on comes from using whatever gifts you are given."

My right side hurt again, and I asked Gretchen if we could continue our talk the next Tuesday.

The Statue

THE BOYS HAD BADLY DISFIGURED me during their attack. This was how I looked when Harold Adams first met me at the garbage facility. He was still staring at me when a big front-end loader pulled up next to him. Dan clambered down from the cab. He was a tall, lanky 29-year-old, with an easy manner and a head of dark curls.

"Harry," he began in a too-loud voice, "What are you fining us for now? You're not giving us another ticket."

"Well, if you would stop keeping paint on the premises," Harry used his "official" voice, "I wouldn't have to write you up. What did you end up doing with those cans?"

"Dumped them down the sewer," Dan said, slyly.

"Sure you did—should have saved some for her," he said, pointing at me. "What's going to happen to her?"

255

"Hell if I know. She was sitting here when we bought the lot from Edmier. I guess they hauled her from a construction job in Forest Park. I have no idea why they kept her. We don't know what to do with her, either. We might move her to the front. Otherwise, she could get stuck in the mud for good. She's a heavy one."

Harold walked around me, looking closely for a clue that would reveal who I was. He crouched down and saw four letters carved into the marble: "ROMA." Straightening up, Harold said, "You know, cleaning up this statue and painting it would be a great project for Robbie's troop. They could earn a community service badge."

"Sounds good to me," Dan said, "but I don't have time to talk about it. Ask Lorraine." He climbed back to his perch in the cab.

Harold walked back to the office to write up his inspection report and have another cup of Lorraine's coffee.

Harold's son Robbie and his fellow scouts were at that tender age of 13. Scouting and sports kept them out of trouble. They were good kids, besides: altar boys serving Sunday Mass. Robbie, Rodger, Eric, Patrick, and John were eighth graders at the neighborhood Catholic school.

When they heard about it, the Scouts weren't crazy about the project Robbie's dad had cooked up for them. Who wanted to paint some old statue at a garbage dump?

The spark in his dad's eyes, though, overcame Robbie's reluctance, as Harold talked about what they were preparing to do to me. "I can borrow the power washer from the firehouse," Harold announced, as he passed the plate of roast pork at the family table. "I'm going to Art's Paint Store downtown to see what would be the best kind."

His wife Adrienne interrupted, "Don't forget to pick up some primer for the bedroom. Why can't we have the boys paint that?" Harold gave her a sharp look. "Because most of it would end up on the floor. No, this will teach them something about ancient times, Egypt—they can say they painted the Queen of the Nile."

The Saturday arrived and the boys gathered at the garbage company dressed in t-shirts and jeans. Rodger stood out from the others with his dark Filipino features. The others were skinny, pale, boys with tousled brown hair.

Harold pulled up with the power washer. Another car parked behind him on Laramie. Dennis Sieron got out with his camera and equipment. Harold had told the local newspaper about the project and they had dispatched Dennis to take photos. They had also assigned the story to a reporter, who interviewed Lorraine and Dan.

"We believe the statue should be placed somewhere in the community," Dan told the reporter, "where it could be appreciated by a large number of residents." He repeated his standing offer to deliver the statue free of charge to any group or individual who had a use for it.

Dan also filled in some history of the statue. "It is believed that it was owned by the commander of the naval base that used to be located in Forest Park."

Lorraine jumped in with an opposing theory. "No, there used to be an animal cemetery there," she countered, "Specifically a cemetery for dogs and horses."

"That's not what I heard," Dan continued in his

257

measured way, "I believe the commander commissioned its building in memory of his horse, which was named Cleopatra. We are not certain if the horse was a pet or a racehorse. We do know Cleopatra was a thoroughbred."

When it came time to write the piece, the reporter, Vince Iaccino, did his homework. He used the first five paragraphs to recount the life of the queen who killed herself at 39, after the Romans betrayed her. He also looked into racing records and found there was a thoroughbred named Cleopatra racing in Chicago during the late 19th century. There was no record of her owner; no mention he was a navy commander.

"We took this place over two-and-half years ago," Dan told the reporter. "The statue was really a sight. It was gradually sinking and we were thinking of getting rid of it. Then Harold came on one of his inspections. He admired the statue and said he would like to restore it. So, we pulled it out of the mud and through his and the Scout's efforts, it will be completely restored."

Lorraine spoke last. "So now we have a beautiful statue with nowhere to go. We would love it if a civic-minded group would take the statue." The article ended with a sentence stating: "Anyone interested in the statue should call 652-0025."

As it turned out, there was only a hint of truth to Dan and Lorraine's account of my history, and the scouts well-intentioned efforts did nothing toward "restoring" me. In their own way, though, they saved me!

First, they pressure-washed me three times, removing clumps of mud and layers of grime. After each wash, I looked a shade whiter, a bit brighter. "Everyone thought it was such a beautiful work," Robbie said, "but there was graffiti and spray paint on it and we couldn't get it off."

Harold provided a gallon of latex-based primer, donated by Art's Paint Store, to cover my stains. The boys dipped their brushes in the white paint and set about covering my blemishes. Just painting me, though, wasn't enough for Harold. He wanted to replace my missing features. The scouts used chisels to chip marble off the back of my throne. They mixed the chips with Crazy Glue and used this concoction to create my new nose. They clumsily reconstructed my breasts, too young to know what real ones looked like. When they completed my makeover, they were very pleased with the results of their hard work. They had no idea that someday it would all need to be undone.

After my makeover, I continued to sit in the yard next to the office. Lorraine tried to interest the local community college, Morton College, in taking me. "I talked to the art instructor about it. But then he left and the interest died out." The library sent someone to look. But, like other local institutions, they didn't have room for me. I seemed destined to live out my days as a curiosity, a shining figure standing out from the rats and refuse.

Edmonia Lewis

OCCASIONAL DAYS OF PAIN TURNED into weeks. I continued my reminiscences with Gretchen on Tuesdays when I felt well enough.

"I told you how sometimes I made things harder for

myself. But there were some injustices—they weren't my fault."

"What happened, Miss Lewis?"

"I'll tell you, but only if you call me Edmonia."

We both laughed. Gretchen continued softly, "All right, Edmonia. You were saying?"

"I have tried to forget these things... to put them away... but they keep creeping back."

"Maybe it would help to talk about them."

Gretchen made it so easy.

"It began with losing my parents. Other children my age had their family to fall back on."

"But you had your mother's family, and Samuel?"

"My Ojibwe family had so many other things to worry about. They had nothing left to give . . . except for my cousin. She cared.

"As for Samuel, he has even more determination than I do. He's made a great success of himself–he earned enough money to pay for my schooling. If it wasn't for him I would never have made it as an artist. But I'm still hurt he got married without telling me."

"Why did he do that? Gretchen shook her head. Her heart felt what was in mine.

"I don't know, but I got over being bitter about it. What happened to me at Oberlin, I couldn't get over. I held onto that pain. I didn't realize my anger . . . it was only hurting me. Until I met Peter. He helped me not to judge all whites. When my anger went away, I felt free. It helped my sculpting."

"You're not angry now, are you?"

"For the most part, I'm content now, but what wounded me the most is no one bought my Cleopatra. You'll never know what she meant to me. Maybe if I weren't colored, Cleopatra would have won an award. She should have at least gotten an honorable mention at the Centennial Exhibition. Then Cleopatra would have found her rightful place in a museum. I wish you could have seen her."

"You talk about her like she was real person."

"If only you knew."

"Whatever happened to it . . .her?"

"I paid a company in Chicago to keep her in storage, but years ago my payment was returned."

I pulled up my blanket as if it could protect me from sorrow. "I don't know what happened to her after that. I don't know where she is."

I turned my head to the wall. Gretchen patted my shoulder.

The Statue

I CONTINUED MY LONELY VIGIL at the garbage facility. The Aichingers had almost given up on finding me a home. Lorraine was looking at me one day, though, when she found a tiny inscription: "E. Lewis." After discovering this new clue, she excitedly pointed it out to Tom. He agreed that it might help them identify the statue, but didn't know where to start.

"She came from Forest Park," Lorraine said excitedly. "Maybe someone there can help us."

She telephoned the Forest Park Public Library and

spoke to Cora Salee. Cora had spent her career collecting newspaper clippings to preserve the village's history. She didn't know what Lorraine was talking about but knew who to ask; her mentor, Dr. Frank J. Orland, the town historian. He had launched the historical society in 1976, as the young country celebrated its second big birthday. When Cora described the statue and its inscriptions to him, Orland consulted the art professor at the university where he taught.

Like my creator, Dr. Orland had been born in upstate New York. He possessed a brilliant mind and was determined to become a doctor or dentist. He moved to Chicago to study at the University of Illinois Medical School. There, he encountered a rare creature: a medical student of the opposite sex. Like the Queen of the Nile, Phyllis was a female pioneer in medicine.

Her comely appearance and kind eyes attracted Frank Orland. The dentist and doctor would marry in 1954 and raise four children.

Frank became a dentist, but, instead of setting up a practice, he concentrated on teaching and research at the University of Chicago. Fascinated by microbiology, he concluded that bacteria caused tooth decay. Other dentists shared his view but Frank took steps to remedy it. He became an early advocate for the fluoridation of water. His four kids walked around with bottles of fluoridated water long before it was fashionable for Americans to carry water bottles.

Seeing that fluoride worked with his kids, he conducted an experiment using two Chicago suburbs to prove his theory. When the test results came in, fluoridation spread across the country.

Now that Dr. Orland had made history, he became obsessed with preserving it. His love for Forest Park led him to collect the arrowheads and jewelry that pioneers plundered from Indian burial mounds. He also chronicled the village's history, but longed for something to put Forest Park on the historical map.

The art professor told Dr. Orland I might be "The Death of Cleopatra" by Edmonia Lewis. Dr. Orland was thrilled. A lost masterpiece had fallen into his hands.

He drove to the garbage facility and looked me over carefully. Satisfied that I was indeed the missing masterpiece, he arranged with Lorraine to move me to Forest Park. Dr. Orland contacted a cemetery and they sent a flatbed truck with a crane. Dr. Orland wrapped me in safety straps. The town's newspaper editor, Bob Haeger, was there to help him, smelling a big story. They drove the truck onto the garbage scale to weigh me (still 3,500 pounds), before heading west.

I arrived back at a familiar place. The torpedo plant was still standing but was now a shopping mall. Dr. Orland was friendly with the owner, Harry Chaddick. He allowed Dr. Orland to lock me away in a storage unit free of charge. I had sat in dark places before.

It was 1985 and Dr. Orland was 69 years old. He was a tall, striking figure, with flyaway white hair and a gray moustache. Dark, rimmed glasses shielded his probing eyes. He consulted with the cemetery's monument maker to see how they should restore me. How appropriate, a merchant of death beautifying my corpse. They spent a few sessions working on me but most of the time they kept me in storage. Dr. Orland was a jealous lover and refused to allow anyone to see me.

Three years after he acquired me, Dr. Orland trumpeted his discovery to the Chicago Tribune. The article ran under the headline, "The Queen of the Nile Sails Home to Forest Park." It was an extensive story, recounting my history. The reporter spoke with my old friend, Harold Adams. "Believe me, I'm just a simple layman," Adams told the newspaper, "but the minute I saw her, I knew the statue was something beautiful. There was graffiti on her breast. So me and the boys gave her a coat of latex—outside white—so she'd look decent until somebody came along who'd know better what to do with her."

Dr. Orland thought he knew better. His discovery captured the attention of author Marilyn Richardson, who had written a book about my sculptor. She flew to Chicago to meet with Dr. Orland. Richardson, an African American, with braided hair, quietly suggested to Dr. Orland that I deserved a wider audience than the people of Forest Park. She thought he should turn me over to an African American museum, or the Smithsonian.

Dr. Orland was outraged in print. "Who is she to come out here and tell us what to do?" He retorted, "This is Forest Park, we know what we're doing here."

"I don't doubt his sincerity," Richardson confided to a reporter, "It's just that he looks at Cleopatra as part of Forest Park history. Somehow, somebody has to make him realize that the sculpture is more than that. It's a priceless part of every American's artistic heritage."

During her visit, Richardson finally persuaded Dr. Orland to allow her to meet me. I basked in her adoring presence, while the Tribune photographer snapped our picture together.

I also came to the attention of the Forest Park Review newspaper. Reporter John Rice interviewed Dr. Orland about his plans for me. Rice became alarmed when the good doctor said he was going to paint me. He intended to use oil-based paint to color my face and arms in "flesh" tones. He planned to paint my robe purple and my bracelets gold. When Rice asked if he could see me, or get a photo for the newspaper, Dr. Orland refused to disclose my whereabouts.

Rice called the Smithsonian and learned they never should paint flesh like mine. He spoke to a curator and urged him to come to Forest Park to free me from Dr. Orland. Rice later wrote an article to stir up controversy about the statue. Dr. Orland fought back, starting an "S.O.S." (Save our Statue) fund. Citizens rallied around and donated money to restore me.

Edmonia Lewis

ON ANOTHER ONE OF OUR visits, I launched into more thoughts about my life. "I hope you don't mind if I reminisce again, Gretchen."

"No, no, Edmonia. Keep talking. I learn something new about you each time. You have kept so much secret from me."

"I thought maybe you wouldn't like me if you knew my darkest secrets," I laughed slightly, knowing my secrets weren't that dark. "I've had only a couple of friends in this world."

"Me too." Gretchen smiled, though, like she didn't mind.

"This time I'm thinking about my angels. Even though I lost loved ones, and was hurt by others, I remember the good people who helped me. I probably haven't thought about them enough. Miss McKagg from my first school, how she loved me even if she couldn't help me. Clara. Reverend Keep and his wife at Oberlin. Mr. Brackett. Even obnoxious Mrs. Child."

"You have talked before about some of these people, but not all."

"If you wouldn't mind, just humor me as I go through the list. My breathing is so bad that I can't explain too much."

"I understand, my dear friend."

"And going back . . . Lloyd Garrison who got me the job with Mr. Brackett. My mentor in Florence . . . oh, what was his name? Even Harriet Hosmer and Miss Cushman. My dear cousin Abequa, the only one who stayed true to me from my Ojibwe family."

"What happened to Abequa?"

"I tried to stay in touch with her. Sent letters. After a couple years, though, the letters came back. My aunts and uncles may be on 'the other side' by now. Abequa is old like me by now. She may be on a reservation—I hope not—or with her French trader."

"Be patient with me as I add to my list. Peter, Mrs. Massri, even the pope."

"The pope?" Gretchen was wide-eyed.

"I told you how he helped me get commissions." I was silent for a while. "Above and beyond all was Samuel. Papa would be proud of how he was a good Haitian brother and helped his little sister."

Gretchen sighed. "Of all of them you have mentioned, Samuel is the one I would like most to meet."

"I'll probably never see him again." I put my hand to my heart, "But he'll always be right here."

"You have had a rich life, Edmonia," Gretchen said.

"I know. And when I think of all the people who helped me, it's almost like good medicine. But there were big spaces between them. In those spaces, my work was my salvation."

I started coughing. Gretchen pulled the covers up to my shoulders, and I fell asleep.

One Tuesday Gretchen surprised me by bringing a doctor to my bedside.

"Hello, Miss Lewis," the tall, handsome young man said, "I'm Dr. Cummings."

Gretchen had brought the doctor without asking me first.

"Yes. I would like to help you, but I need to know what your symptoms are. Where does it hurt?"

I almost laughed. "That covers a lot of territory, Doctor. Gretchen, you don't have to hear all this."

"No, I want to," Gretchen said, as she took a chair and sat by my bed.

"Sometimes I get fevers. Sometimes my back hurts. You can see that my face is swollen. My feet are also swelling. I can barely get my shoes on."

"Where do you experience the most pain?" the doctor asked.

"On my right side and under my ribs. It comes and goes."

Dr. Cummings' face fell ever so slightly. He took out his stethoscope. "Your heart is beating rapidly."

We were all quiet for a moment. Gretchen took my hand and squeezed it.

"We have to rule out Bright's disease," the young doctor finally said. "We treat it through hot baths, bed rest, and sometimes blood-letting to bring down the blood pressure."

"Ooh," Gretchen and I reacted together.

"You still bleed people?" I asked in amazement. "Will I die from this?"

"You may, but you will probably live for several more years."

"I don't know if that's good or bad news." I laughed like it was a joke.

Gretchen forced a smile, but her chin trembled.

"Try hot baths and bed rest for now, Miss Lewis, and I'll check on you in a few weeks."

After he left, Gretchen sobbed, "You're too young."

"I'm not that young. In another year, I'll be sixty."

I loved Gretchen holding my hand and patting my forehead with a cold cloth, but I needed to be alone.

"Thank you for bringing the doctor . . . I guess," I

attempted a little laugh. "But I need some time. I have a lot to think about."

My sunny-haired friend kissed my forehead and left.

The Statue

LIKE MY CREATOR, I WAS now under a doctor's care, but he seemed more like a mad scientist. Smithsonian curator George Gurney began corresponding with Dr. Orland. They wrestled over my fate. In the meantime, Gurney had compiled an accurate account of my history. "Lewis had had an African American patron in Chicago. She brought it from Philadelphia and displayed the statue at an annual exhibition. The patron apparently didn't buy it, so it was placed in storage. The fees went unpaid, so the warehouse took possession. It somehow ended up in a bar." He had no idea that I had also spent many years as a gravestone for a horse.

In September 1988, Gurney flew to Chicago to see me. He was a slender six-footer, with a dignified manner, and very measured way of speaking. When he asked to examine me, Dr. Orland gave his usual response; "The Queen's not ready to be seen." Having traveled such a distance, Gurney finally obtained his permission to view me.

After he saw me, Gurney told a reporter, "It is a shadow of what was done originally. The statue is badly damaged and weathered. Portions cannot be redone because the detail is gone. Major restoration would cost a lot of money."

Gurney looked at my blue and green paint stains. He examined the "well-intentioned but unprofessional attempt at restoration" by the Boy Scouts.

"The creamy white paint they used was slightly more yellowish than the original marble."

Gurney had the nerve to say this paint made my flesh look like "plastic."

"The paint was so off-putting," he lamented. He was hopeful, though, because, "Everything is reversible about their restoration."

Despite my pitiful state, Christie's still valued me at $150,000. Gurney saw me as an object of historic importance and believed the Smithsonian could save me. The museum had experts in this field and could call in outside consultants. He believed I should take my rightful place in the National Museum of American Art, surrounded by other works of my creator; *Hagar* and *The Old Arrow Maker.*

Back in Washington, Gurney found the only photo of how I originally looked. "Now I knew the 'restored' asp and hands were totally incorrect. I didn't know how we could restore the breasts. The paint had to be stripped off."

Misdirected as they were, Gurney credited the Boy Scouts with saving my life. "That thick paint was the only thing that was holding the marble together." He was confident they could restore my sandals and headdress, if Dr. Orland would release the statue to him. I was caught in a tug of war between the historical society and the Smithsonian for the next seven years.

During one of Gurney's visits to Forest Park, it finally came to a head. Frank Orland was approaching 76 and had grown more cantankerous with the years. Gurney tried to reason with him.

"Listen, your historical society doesn't have the money to restore her. It's not a job for amateurs. You also don't have a place to display her. We can do the job right and exhibit her in the place where she belongs."

Dr. Orland suddenly slumped like a tired old man, beaten down by the war of words with Gurney, and knowing he had made minute progress with his own restoration. "You're right," he admitted. "The membership of the historical society is dwindling. We've got no place to put it. I'm willing to give it to you for transportation costs."

Gurney was relieved. "Don't worry, Frank, we'll take good care of her. We'll also make it clear to visitors that she is a gift from the Forest Park Historical Society. You deserve credit for saving her."

The good Doctor Orland had failed to nurse me back to health, but at least he put me in the hands of a specialist.

Before the Smithsonian shipped me to Washington, my restoration needed to be completed. Gurney assigned the job to a rising star in the world of sculpture conservation.

Andrzej Dajnowski was 37 when he met me. He lived in Chicago, where he was responsible for restoring the many statues that graced its parks. He also worked for the Art Institute and took on the most prominent pieces in the city. He had studied conservation and sculpture in his native Poland.

Andrzej had immigrated to the U.S. in 1985 to continue his conservation studies at Harvard University. He later received his PhD from Copernicus University in Poland. The conservator made a big splash when he pioneered the laser cleaning of buildings and sculptures. There was demand for his services from Cairo to Canada. I would present one of his greatest challenges.

Edmonia Lewis

AFTER GRETCHEN LEFT, I DIDN'T feel as disheartened as I expected. To my surprise, the lovely coolness returned. It had such power that it cast out my fever. It stayed with me the longest time ever, perhaps 15 minutes. Peacefully, I drifted off to sleep.

That night I dreamed. Everything was swirling around me. Amidst the swirling, my father was giving me one of his broad smiles. Round and round he went, until he grabbed that familiar wooden cross with the chains. "I told you how a Lwa could help you in the crossroads of life. Who do you think was protecting you during your frightening voyages? Your canoe trip on the Erie? Your train ride across the Alps? Do you remember the first time you felt that gust of wind? Can you understand now that it was Baron Samedi, sent by me, who came to you when you reached the crossroads of your life?"

Then I saw my mother, as strong and serious as ever. She joined my father in the crazy swirling and said, "All those times you wondered who was saying, 'I will be with you, Mary. I will always be with you.' That was me, my child. I gave you your greatest gift, your power to create. My spirit came to you when you were loneliest. You were never an orphan. I was always with you."

And then came Cleopatra. As she swirled around, her throne kept bumping into my mother and father. "No, I wasn't behind the wind and the loving words,

272

but it was I who sent you the visions of the hand and of me sitting on the throne. It was I who told you to go to Rome and who told you not to give up. And, of course, it was I who sent the cool rippling that even tonight brought you joy. Your mother's and father's spirits played their part in keeping you going, but your crowning accomplishment came from me and my ghost: The Ghost of Cleopatra."

As Dr. Cummings predicted, I lived several more years. I had some good days but mostly bad ones. My solace was that I finally felt secure. My mother's words, my father's protection, and The Ghost of Cleopatra had made my happiness possible, along with the devotion of a young white woman.

When I was near the end, Gretchen brought me to the Hammersmith Borough Infirmary. I told the doctors that I was only 44. They laughed. I told Gretchen I was leaving her a healthy inheritance. She said she would use it to go to the University of Vienna and take classes from Dr. Freud. The way she listened to me so intently, I wasn't surprised she wanted to become a psychoanalyst.

I discussed my last wishes with her. I wanted a Catholic nun to supervise the preparations for my burial, and my body to be enclosed in a dark walnut coffin. I asked that the funeral service take place in the Catholic Church of Our Lady of Victories, Kensington. Then I wanted my body brought to the Kensal Green Catholic Cemetery on a carriage draped to hide my coffin from view. No one knew when I came to this earth, and no one would know when I left.

The Statue

WORKERS PACKED ME INTO A truck. The museum insured me for $100,000 and shipped me to a garage on Chicago's northwest side. It was a modest structure, with some unusual features; skylights and large windows that flooded it with sunlight.

Andrzej had a handsome face, topped by graying hair. There was a determined look in his eyes. The Smithsonian had commissioned him to fix me.

"George contacted me and asked if I wanted to work on it," he recalled. "The statue was brought to me. It was very heavy." When he looked at me, he could tell the Boy Scouts had used some sharp object to chip marble off the back of my throne. "They mixed it with epoxy in a very sloppy attempt to restore her features. They cut off her sandals," he said with a frown. "They never should have been allowed to work on it."

Restoring my missing features wasn't the most difficult part. "The face had dark paint on it. I applied solvents to dissolve the paint and used clay to absorb the stain." He "pulled" the stains from my marble using this poultice. After he removed my "makeup," he could see my complexion. "It was a bit sugary," he recalled. "Some detail was lost but it wasn't horrible. Considering what the marble had gone through, it was amazing what was left."

After Andrzej undid the makeshift repairs the Boy Scouts had made. I looked positively grotesque—a decomposed corpse.

Working from the photograph George Gurney had given him, the conservator gave me back my nose. He fixed my lips and restored my shattered chin. He used a large fill to restore my right and left breasts.

My left hand, the one Allegra had dangled from the chair, had to be completely rebuilt. My right hand also required a great deal of work. Andrzej reconstructed the venomous head of the serpent. He filled the numerous holes in my robe and restored the delicate decorations missing from my sandals. He fixed my vulture headdress and filled in the missing marble on the back of my throne.

It took him nine months to return me to my former grandeur. His son, Bartosz, was 12 and a frequent visitor to the garage. He watched his father, a master craftsman at work. It was inspiring for him to see my beauty re-emerge under his father's hands. He would later join his dad in the family business, also becoming a laser expert.

The whole job had cost the Smithsonian $30,000. When Andrzej visited the museum, his colleagues spoke in wonder about the miracle he had performed. Bartosz came to visit me. My radiance amazed him.

Here I sit in the American Museum of Art, where I dominate the room. I am the Queen once again, and millions come to worship me on my throne. My sculptor's other works surround me.

I'm resting on a dark wooden pedestal. It bears a plaque: "A Gift from the Forest Park Historical Society." Dr. Orland, who died in 2000, had lived to see me in my rightful place.

"No one in the Historical Society had the same level

of interest," George Gurney recalled. "He wanted to make sure the statue was preserved after his death. We will never place her in storage. Certain iconic characters like Cleopatra will always be on display."

If you are ever in Washington, stop by to pay me tribute. It is not my wish but my command!

Afterword

JOHN RICE AND I WORKED together to write a book about Edmonia Lewis, because we both felt strongly that our subject deserved to be brought to the public's attention . . . again. I wrote the sections where Edmonia speaks, and John wrote the parts where Cleopatra and the Statue speak.

We did a great deal of research, and of utmost assistance to us in our research was Jean Marie Pierre, a first-generation immigrant from Haiti. He enlightened me about the culture of Haiti, the homeland of Edmonia's father. He did extensive research on nineteenth century transportation. Over and over again we were amazed that Edmonia Lewis had the courage to handle all of its rigors—especially being alone, young, and a woman of color. Jean Pierre also traveled to Washington, DC, to get a firsthand look at Edmonia's Cleopatra.

I studied the biographies of Edmonia Lewis written by Harry Henderson, Albert Henderson, Romare Bearden, Kirsten Pi Buck, and Marilyn Richardson. Each of these individuals recorded any facts he or she could discover about our subject. However, facts have always been hard to come by because Edmonia was vague about her background. She chose to be a mystery. Within recent years, Marilyn Richardson did find out the exact grave--- C350---where Edmonia was buried in 1907. It was covered with a slab of stone bare of any writing. Shortly before the publication of this book, I inquired with the cemetery and they said that through fund raising from America there is a new plaque with Edmonia's name on it describing her as a famous sculptor from America. Alas, Edmonia is beginning to be recognized again.

Oberlin College was helpful before we even planned to write the book. Since the statue had been in Forest Park for so long, and the Historical Society wanted to know about its history, they contacted Oberlin several times. Oberlin sent copies of classes taken by Edmonia, local news articles about the poison charges, and information about the Keeps' residential home.

I sought information and insights from Valerie Mercer, curator of African American Art at the Detroit Institute of Art. She led me to a little-known photograph of Edmonia and some fresh insights into her work. Afterwards, I had the privilege of viewing two of Edmonia Lewis' sculptures at the DIA. Dan Ward, curator of the Erie Canal Museum, told me a great deal about the locks and directed me to the museum's informative website. I contacted Carl Kimberly, curator of the now defunct New York Central College. Mr. Kimberly wanted me to give special mention to Catherine Hanchett whose speeches about the college he shared with me. Sadly, Mr. Kimberly passed away about a year after I spoke with him, but in his old age, he was still very proud of New York Central.

Matt Wilkinson from The Mississauga Heritage Society in Ontario educated me about the Credit River Reservation, the John Mike family and the sincere, although perhaps misguided, efforts of Reverend Peter Jones to rescue the Canadian Ojibwe in the 1800s. Jackie, an Ojibwe historian from the Sioux Saint Marie Cultural Center, shared detailed information about the customs of her people, including the spirit houses and leather wristbands which adults still affix to their children's wrists after a loved one dies.

Almost all of the characters in the book are real. But unlike a purely historical novel, historical fiction seeks to help the reader get into a person's soul and thereby reveal what it felt like to be that person in her particular time and place. To do this, we sometimes add characters with whom the subject speaks and interacts. In regards to Edmonia, the additional characters I added are Miss McKagg, Elisabeth from Miss Cushman's group, Peter at the Vatican, the names of the girls at New York Central and the names of Edmonia's aunts and uncles. "Abequa" was added in the hope that at least one survivor of Edmonia's Ojibwe family still showed tenderness for her. However, in an interview, Edmonia talked about how her family was very cold when she returned to visit them. I assume that was because every year that Edmonia was gone the White Man forced them to give up more of their preferred life, and they may have become bitter.

Another fictional character is Mrs. Massri. Regarding Edmonia's possible trip to Paris, one source said there is evidence that Edmonia Lewis' name was on the guest list of a Paris hotel after the time when she created her best work. We do not know whether or not she went there to research new trends in art or if she visited Rodin's studio.

Edmonia's German friend in London is based on Edmonia's own written reference to the daughter of a

German baker. Edmonia did make the final plans for her funeral and burial. She did leave some money to the baker's daughter.

During my research, I formed my own understanding of Edmonia's determination and creativity as well as her loneliness from feeling like an outsider. The voice I've given Edmonia is from my interpretation of her persona.

Gail Tanzer

I have been researching Edmonia Lewis and her statue, *The Death of Cleopatra*, for a quarter century. I first encountered the story in 1992. I was a crusading newspaper reporter who became concerned about the statue's fate in the care of Dr. Frank Orland. I wrote about the controversy on February 19, 1992, advocating for the Smithsonian to take possession of the statue.

As a member of the Forest Park Historical Society, I had access to our archives concerning Edmonia and her statue. Among these was a newspaper photograph of the Boy Scouts painting the statue. This enabled me to locate and interview three of them. I also had regular conversations with Dr. Orland about the statue, though he would not permit me to see her.

I later contacted Oberlin College and obtained a complete copy of their archives on Edmonia. These documents were invaluable for piecing together her college career and her criminal trial.

After Gail and I began work on the book, I read "Stories in Stone," a book by David B. Williams that told me all I needed to know about the geologic formation of marble and how it was harvested. To capture the story of Cleopatra, I read "Cleopatra the Great" by Dr. Joann Fletcher and "Cleopatra: A Biography" by Duane W. Roller.

I used my investigative skills to locate and interview every person I could identify as having contact with the statue. These included the property owners of the excavation company and garbage facility where the statue languished for so long. I also interviewed the newspapermen who covered the restoration of the statue. Finally, I interviewed the conservator, Andrzej Dajnowski, and his son, Bartosz, about the complete restoration.

Our researcher, Jean Marie Pierre, conducted a crucial interview with Curator Emeritus George Gurney in Washington, DC. This allowed me to recreate the negotiations between the Smithsonian and Dr. Orland.

In telling this story, though, it was necessary to create some fictional characters. These include the cavatori, the crew of the Bella Sposa and the model, Allegra. The character Seamus Delaney is also fictional. Everyone else in my accounts of Cleopatra and the statue are real people.

The horses Alixir and Bucephalus were also made up. As for the filly Cleopatra, we know she was a thoroughbred owned by Blind John Condon. We also know she raced in the early twentieth century at Chicago-area racetracks. We do not know how she died but I borrowed the story of the late filly, Ruffian, to describe that scene.

When it came to writing from the statue's point of view, I received invaluable help from my French writing students at the INSEEC Business School. They taught me to write about the statue with the utmost emotion. They fell in love with Edmonia and her statue like I did. In my lifetime of writing, I've never found a better story.

John Rice